D1527817

I Got Love for My Shawty 2

Tina Jenkins

@ Instagram MSTJADAMS

@ Twitter   jenkinstina72

@ Facebook Author T Jenkins

Text Shan to 22828 to stay up to date with new releases, sneak peeks, contest, and more…

Check your spam if you don't receive an email thanking you for signing up.

Table of Contents

Alicia

It had been a week, and I couldn't believe that that motherfucker shot me and was able to walk away without a scratch. That was okay. I had something for that ass; he had better hoped and prayed that someone else got to him first. That nigga got the game fucked up, if he thought I was going to let that shit ride, brother-in-law, or not.

I needed to get up out of that hospital bed, so that I could get out there and look for him. I threw the covers over and stood up to get my clothes out the locker.

"Baby, what are you doing? You know, damn well, you can't leave the hospital, yet." Cornell said, helping me back to the bed.

"I can't sit in here, while your brother is out there like a fucking maniac. Not only did he shoot me, he is not finished with Jasmine; you heard what your mother said. Everything was similar except for the makeshift grave, which is probably already made; he's just waiting to catch her." I cried in his arms.

"Baby, listen. I know it seems like nothing is happening fast enough, but believe me when I say, there is a plan in play already, and he won't be on this earth to bother anyone in due time. We just have to wait for things to fall into place, without getting caught up. Mo was right when he said that no mistakes could be made, because it would've been defeating the purpose, if he lived."

"I need to see my sisters. Can you please call them?"

"Bitch, we already here. We would be here more, but your damn husband hogging the hospital room." Candace stuck her tongue out at Cornell, who put his hands up to surrender.

"Baby, I know better than to get into it with four women, so I'll head out, and I'll be back later."

"Four women, it's only three of us." I said before Mike's friend, Jessica, walked in with Jasmine, holding four coffees from Dunkin Donuts.

"Well, well, well. What do we have here my two sisters?" I asked, rubbing my hands together.

"Hi, I'm Jessica, Mike's girlfriend. I met you at the dinner you had at your house, and unfortunately, when you had this situation happen to you."

"Girl, Mike's sneaky ass been messing with her for over two months, now, and didn't say shit to nobody. Evidently, over the last week, they been fucking the shit out of each other, and Mike made her his girl, which means that he is feeling her more than we know, or that her ass got that fire pussy like us." Candace said, with her ignorant ass, laughing hard, as hell.

"Wait until I see Mike. I see he got himself a Puerto Rican chick, huh? Let's just say that I know Spanish, too, so don't let me hear you talking shit about my brother in another language." Alicia said, rolling her eyes at Jessica.

"Cut the shit, Alicia. Damn. She cool, as hell, and Mike will expect you to treat her with respect, so don't do it to yourself. You remember how pissed he was with you when you cussed his fake ass baby mom out.

"Fuck that bitch! If she didn't bounce to Texas, I would've killed her myself."

"Well, that's your ass if some shit pops off. Anyway, when they discharging your ass?" Candace asked.

"I don't know, but I'm ready to go; I can tell you that. I feel better already. Fuck that nigga. You know, I never thought that nigga was capable of something like this with his corny ass. But, I guess, you can't judge a book by its cover, right?"

"Well, Jessica, I know these two fools grilled you already, and Mike must've put you through his weird ass series of tests, if you hanging with these two bitches." I said, sticking up my middle fingers, with them doing the same, in return. But, if you are who Mike chose, then I will respect that. I'm just telling you not to hurt him; he will not take it, lightly, just because you're good in bed. These men that we have are not what you're used to.

My husband is a different story, but something tells me that that's going to change by how tight they've become. I won't go into details about what. Just know that it takes a good woman to get your man to where you want him to be, and it does start in the bedroom. It's, obviously, working thus far for you in that department, because I heard that he had just got you a new truck. Now, it doesn't matter that you didn't ask for it; that's the kind of man he is.

But, a word of caution. A hurt man is like a scorned woman. A hurt man will do the unthinkable; they will do horrible things to you. Things you only see in movies, and it's hard; there's no escaping. Just ask Jasmine, if you don't believe me; she is, definitely, dealing with a hurt man."

"Thank you, ladies, for all of the insight on Mike, and I will take heed to your warning. I am not a woman who sleeps around, and to be honest, he is the first man I've been with since my fiancé. I'm shocked that he was able to get into my mind, spirit, and heart the way that he has already. I don't know if I was looking for love, or if he just fell into my lap. I will never tell him I love him until he tells me, because I don't want to scare him away."

"You are in love with Mike?" I asked, waiting to see her reaction.

She blushed and smiled before answering, "Yes, I think it happened when I didn't expect it to, and when we had sex, it just sealed the deal. Every time I think about sex with that man, I get turned on. Whew! Anyway, I can't say it's a rebound love, because I've been single for two years.

He really touched my heart with all the little things he says and does for me. For instance, I was at work the other day, and he sent me a text telling me that he was thinking about me and that he couldn't wait to see me. Another one was bringing me flowers and coming to have lunch with me. The best one was that he wanted to meet my son, and when he did, he treated him like his own. It's the little things that get me to love you, not buying me shit that I could buy myself. Everything about him is so genuine, but don't tell him I told you about the texts; he may get embarrassed."

"Damn, girl, that nigga got you sprung. It's good to know you feel that way, though. It's been a long time for him, as well." Jasmine said.

"Well, welcome to the family." I told her, as Mike and Mo walked in together.

"Hey, Mike. I talked to your girl, and I must say, I'm impressed. I didn't think you had it in you to pick a good one." I told him, as he kissed me on the cheek.

"You have to excuse them, baby. Alicia is the mean one, Candace is the ignorant one, and Jasmine used to be the stuck-up one, until Mo bust that ass and knocked that shit out of her." Mike said, laughing, while he and Mo gave each other a pound.

"Oh, really? Mo, you knocked it out of me?" Jasmine whined.

"Oh, come here, baby. You know daddy bust that ass on a regular basis, and I did knock it out of you." Mo said, pulling her close and kissing her.

"Ok, it's time to talk about what we are really here for. It's time for us to get that nigga, but we are going to need y'all help, so close the door, while we discuss it." Darrell and Cornell walked in right after he said it; they were talking about sports, as usual.

"Baby, I'll wait for you outside." Jessica told Mike, walking out the door. Mike walked up behind her, held her waist, and whispered into her ear, making her giggle. Everybody just looked at the two of them acting like teenagers.

"Do y'all mind if Jess is in here?" Mike asked.

Everybody looked at Mike like he was crazy before Candace ignorant ass said, "Girl, get your ass over here. You're Mike's woman, and whether you like it, or not, you in this shit with us. Now, let's talk about how the fuck we gone get this nigga."

Mike

After we came back from the hospital discussing what we were going to do, I drove Jess to my mom's house so that they could finally meet. My mom kept asking when she was going to meet the woman that had been keeping me away from her. Jessica was a little nervous, but I kissed the back of her hand and told her that my mom was going to love her. We pulled up to my mom's house and noticed that she and Ms. D was sitting out on the front porch, smoking cigarettes and playing cards. I took Jess's hand and started walking up to my house to introduce them.

"Mom, this is Jessica Gomez. The woman I told you about, and who you keep complaining that is keeping me away from you. And Ms. D, you two have already met. " I told her, reaching in to give both of them a kiss.

"Well, she sure is pretty, Mike. Wait a minute, where do I know you from?" She quizzed Jess, but I already knew what was coming next.

"Hi, Ms. Watson. I work at the hospital with you, but I didn't know he was your son." She told my mom, squeezing my hand.

"Hold on, don't you have a baby by Dr. Fisher? D, this is the girl I told you about two years ago that found her doctor fiancé was fucking some chic in one of the rooms.

They used to sleep in-between shifts. That nigga was foul?"
She said, as if Jessica wasn't standing there.

"Get the fuck out of here. I remember that story; I
couldn't understand why you just walked away. Back in my
day, we all would've been fired, and I would've whipped her
ass every time I saw her after that." Ms. D said, smoking her
cigarette.

"Well, it's nice to meet you, anyway. Don't act like you
don't know me when that doctor nigga around either. If
you're going to be with my son, don't be ashamed of what
you have. He is a good man, and I won't allow any woman to
come and turn him into something he's not over some
pussy." My mom said, extending her hand to shake it.

"I know that's fucking right." Ms. D chimed in,
plucking her ashes on the ground.

I grabbed Jess's hand and took her into the house. I
could tell that she was embarrassed and upset by how red her
faced had turned.

"Baby, you have to stop letting people get to you. I
know she's my mom, but if I thought she was disrespecting
you, I would've said something to her. She is just fucking with
you; that's how she is. You'll get to know her and laugh this
off. Do you want to leave and go get something to eat?"

"No, we can eat here."

"I don't want you to feel uncomfortable in any way." I
told her, before letting her hand go to walk into the kitchen.

As I walked in the kitchen, Jess went to sit on the couch and waited for me to make her a plate. I came out with the food and noticed her crying, as she hung the phone up. I put the plate down and ran over to her to see what the hell had happened just that quick.

"Baby, what's wrong? Who was that on the phone?" I quizzed her, now getting nervous. I had to pull her close to me, because she was becoming hysterical, as she tried to speak. "Jess, what's wrong? Please tell me; you're scaring me." I looked in her eyes worried as hell.

"What's going on in here? Mike, what the fuck you do? Why is she crying like that?" My mom asked, with Ms. D right behind her.

"Move boy." My mom said, pushing me out the way. Ms. D slapped me upside the back of my head and sat on the other side of her, while I just stood there against the wall watching her cry.

"I know we got off to a rough start, but if you're going to be around, you have to talk to me. So, what's the matter? Why are you crying like that?" My mom asked, hugging her, now, with Ms. D rubbing her back.

"Mike, go get her some tissue, dammit." Ms. D yelled out at me.

"That was my doctor's office on the phone, and she just told me I'm pregnant." She said, looking up at me.

"Ok, well what's wrong with that? If you and this nigga was fucking without protection, what did you expect?" My mom asked her.

"Mike and I are in a good space right now. We both live hectic lives and bringing another kid into the equation is going to complicate things. I'm scared of having another child with a disability, which can happen again. There's no way I can keep this baby." She was crying, still trying to talk.

"It's going to be ok, baby. It would be great to have you and Jasmine have my grandbabies around the same time. I mean, she should be, what, almost two months now? How far along are you?" My mom asked, looking back at me like she was aggravated and not happy.

"I'm not sure, yet. I go for my first appointment next week, but it shouldn't be more than a couple weeks. I mean, we just had sex for the first time about that long ago. I know we should've been using protection, but if I can be honest with you; it felt better without it." She laughed, as she said it.

"Oh, no she didn't. Well, girl listen, most dicks do feel better without the condom, but this is what you get for trying to have that feeling. So, now you and Mike need to decide what you're going to do, because that baby didn't ask to be here. It would be a shame to make him or her suffer, because your asses couldn't or, should I say, wouldn't cover it up." My mom said. Her and Ms. D got up and walked into the kitchen talking shit to me like I was the only one involved.

"Baby, what do you want to do? I know it's early, and we should've been more careful, but because we weren't, it's our fault. I don't want you to kill my baby, but if that's something you need to do, I'll support you. The only thing I ask is that you make that decision on not really being ready for a baby, and not because you think he or she will have a disability. I'm not worried about that; you should know that my family is tight as hell, and you will always have help.

Matter of fact, let's go so we can discuss this at home, but I'm making you a plate. Your ass will eat for two until you decide what you want to do." I told her, walking into the kitchen to get foil to wrap the plates up.

"Mike, are you sure that's your baby?" My mom asked me, with a serious face. I was mad as hell that she asked me that, but I understood why she did.

"Yes, that's my baby. I've been with her every day, and I knew it was a chance that she could get pregnant, but I didn't think it would happen that fast." I told them.

"Negro, that's y'all problem. You know, damn well, being with her every day doesn't mean shit. Look what happened with that other girl, and she left with my grandbaby, and ain't nobody seen her since." My mom yelled at me.

"Really, Ma? That wasn't even my baby, and you acting like he was. I mean, I did too, but she had every right to bounce; she didn't owe us anything. When she first left two years ago, I found her and asked her to come back, and she refused, so I let it be.

11

I'm positive this is my baby, and I hope she does decides to keep it, but I'm going to support her no matter what choice she makes. And I expect you to do the same, and show her some respect. Your ass in here comparing her to that trifling ass chic. Come on, Ma. That's my woman, and I won't have you or no one else treat her any way. She is only the second girl I ever introduced you to, and you did the same shit. And Ms. D, you never treated Candace like that, so can you have my back on this." I kissed both of them on the cheek, grabbed Jess's hand, and walked out, mad as hell that they were acting like that.

Jessica

I was going to meet Mike's mom, and I was nervous as hell. If this was the same lady from the hospital, she was a bitch, and if she didn't like you, she would fuck with you. I made sure I spoke to her ass every day and kept it moving. I was not one of those drama-filled girls, and I wasn't going to be one because somebody always had a chip on their shoulder.

As soon as we walked up, I could see her face turned up, and I didn't even get to the porch yet. I wondered if her mean ass recognized me from the hospital without me saying anything. Fuck, she did, and that was not a happy welcome. It was unpleasant just as I suspected, but I would never disrespect his mom. Mike knew how uncomfortable I was, so he grabbed my hand and took me into the house to make a plate. As he made the plates, my phone started ringing, and I knew who the caller was, because she did me a favor.

"Hey, Laura, please tell me you have some good news, and that it's just a cold." I prayed, talking into the phone.

"Ugh, no bitch, your ass is pregnant. How the fuck did that happen, when you basically just met that nigga? Yo, you got a winner, though, so keep him happy, before somebody snatches him up." She said, before hanging the phone up. I had to look at my phone, because I could've sworn that she was warning me of

something, but I nixed it off. Out of the blue, I just started crying hysterically, when his mom and her mean ass friend walked in, acting like they care.

When I told them, it appeared as if they were genuinely concerned, until I heard his mother go into the kitchen and start talking shit. His mom really didn't give a fuck; asking him if it was his baby, and basically, saying I slept around in so many words. Who the hell did she think she was?

I was happy when Mike said something about her disrespecting me. He didn't lie when he said he would always have my back, and I guess that included with his mom, too. I felt bad that he had to go in on her for me, but her evil ass deserved it. I couldn't help but wonder if Jasmine went through the same thing when she met her. I was definitely going to talk to her about that shit and what she did. I know that that's his mom and that's her son, but I won't tolerate that shit again. He will always choose his mom, and I'm ok with that, because my son will be the same way, but he needs to make sure that she stays in her place.

The car ride home was pretty quiet. I was looking out of the window, and Mike and I hadn't said two words to each other. I know that it wasn't his fault and that he had my back, but I needed time to think about what I was going to do. We were stopped at a light, when I turned the radio up to blast the song "Weak" by SWV.

I don't know what it is that you've done to me,

But it's ok to act in such a crazy way,
Whatever it is, that you do, when you what you doing,
it's a feeling I want to stay,

He just smiled and placed one of his perfect kisses on my lips when the car behind us blew to let us know the light had changed. I was glad that that song came on, because I was feeling that way every day for him, and I didn't want him to think that I was mad. I heard his phone vibrate, and Mo's name popped up, so he answered through the Bluetooth.

"What it do, bro?" He said and grabbed my hand, kissing the back of it.

"Shit, my nigga. We all over here at the bar, playing pool. I wanted to see if you were up to a game. And bring Jessica with you." Jasmine yelled in the background. It's girls against the guys, and we need another girl if you come." He looked over at me, and I shook my head no, because I just wanted to go home after finding out the news of being someone else's mom.

"Nah, we staying in tonight, but I got you tomorrow." He said, before saying their goodbyes.

"Baby, I don't want you to stay in because of me. Go have fun with your family." I told him.

"That's ok. They know I have a woman now, so I can't be with them all the time like before." He said, pulling up in front of my house.

We walked into my mom's house to get Damien, and she could already tell that something was wrong. She gave me a hug, and I started crying right away, so she asked Mike what happened.

"I think she should tell you. It's not bad if you ask me, but she thinks it is."

"I'm pregnant, Ma." I told her, laying down on her lap. I was really a mama's girl, and if Mike didn't know, he knew now.

"Baby, that's ok. Why are you crying? Is something wrong with the baby? Wait, is it Mike's?" She quizzed me, looking over her glasses.

"Why does everybody keep asking if it's Mike's? I haven't been with anyone else, Ma. You should know better than anyone. Mike and I only been together a few months, and I don't think we're ready. Especially, with Damien having Down Syndrome. I'm scared that it will happen again."

"I'm ready for a baby, shit; I want her to keep it. That's her decision, though; I'm going to have her back regardless. I'm going to get Damien and take him upstairs to put him to bed. It's late, unless you keeping him for the night?" He said.

"No baby. I want him to come upstairs tonight. Can you take him up there? The keys are over on the table. I'll be up in a minute." I told him, watching him walk out with my son.

"Jessy, you need to stop thinking like that. Just because you're pregnant again, doesn't mean the baby will be disabled. If you want to keep the baby, you know I'll be there to help,

16

and I'm sure he has a mom. You told me that he had three sisters, two with kids, and another has one on the way. I mean, shit, the baby is going to have a huge family already, so stop being selfish to yourself, Mike, and most of all, the baby. I love you, but you know that, even though you may not go to church like you used to, abortion is a sin." She made sure to say, as I walked out of the door.

"I know it's a sin." I mumbled underneath my breath, making sure she didn't hear me get smart.

"I put my stuff down on the counter and watched Mike rock Damien back to sleep. I ran to get my phone and snapped a picture to save as my screensaver. I posted it on Instagram and added the caption, *"Both of my men. I couldn't ask for anything more."* Mike turned around and saw me standing there leaning against the wall watching him.

He laid Damien in his crib and walked over to me. "Are you sure you don't want to keep the baby? I don't want to pressure you, but if you don't, I know it's not a good idea to wait until you're too far to get it. And I'm not sure if, after the first appointment, I would let you once I hear the heartbeat. Yes, I know all about it from Candace, Alicia, and now, Jasmine. Please let me know before the doctor's appointment, because I'm going, and if you're not keeping it, then there's no need to go." He said, holding me from behind, then walking out the room.

"I am going to think about it. Can you give me a few days? I will definitely let you know before the appointment next week. Until then, go hang out with your family. I'm not going anywhere. I'll be here writing a paper and waiting for you to come home." I told him, grabbing his dick.

"Fuck! You can have your dick now. I can go out another time." He said, getting ready to undress.

"No, I have a paper to write. Text me when you on your way back. I may have a surprise for you." I whispered in his ear, sticking my tongue in, knowing that it was his spot.

"You play too much, Jess. I want my surprise when I come back." He said, kissing me on the way out. I watched him walk to the car in his black thermal shirt, black jeans, black Timbs, and his gold chain that he always wore around his neck. *Damn, that man is fine, and thank goodness he is mines. Whew! I can't wait until he comes back. Shit, that's why I'm pregnant now. Let me get this damn paper done, or at least, start it.*

I looked at my phone first, pulled up Instagram, and saw how many likes I got. Of course, Candace's ass commented at the bottom, "Stop being so mushy for a few minutes and come have a damn drink."

Mike must've looked when he got in his car because he posted, *"And I couldn't have asked for a better family."* I just smiled and put my phone down to start writing.

Alicia

I finally got released from the hospital a week ago, but now, I wanted to get out of the house. I was feeling cooped up, so I had Candace come pick me up, because we all made plans to go to the bar and shoot pool. I text Cornell to meet us at the bar when he got off work. When we pulled in the parking lot, Mike pulled up at the same time smoking a blunt. We walked over, sat in his car and smoked, before going in. It was mad people at the bar that night, but you couldn't tell from outside, because there were barely any cars there. We found Jasmine, Mo, and Darrell over by the pool table and walked over.

"Oh shit! Bitch, I didn't know you were coming. I thought we were going to have a girls against guys team, but Jessica didn't want to come out, so it's going to be uneven. But, fuck it." Jasmine said, sitting on Mo's lap, watching Darrell take his turn. Cornell walked in not too long after we got there, taking his jacket off like he was about to win against my sisters and me.

The music was playing on the jukebox and we were having a good old time, when I noticed that bitch over at the bar pointing in the direction that we were sitting. I couldn't tell who she was pointing at until Mike stood up. The song "Anaconda" came on by Nicki, and she got out of her seat doing some nasty ass dance. I guess, trying to get Mike's attention, who wasn't paying her no mind. He was too focused on trying to beat us. When his turn was finished, I walked over to him, sitting on the stool, while drinking a beer.

"Yo', brother, who the hell is that bitch staring at you and dancing extra hard trying to get your attention? I mean, if I didn't know any better, I would've thought you fucked her or promised her something." I told him, grabbing my beer and sitting on the stool next to him.

"That's some chic that was in the bar with Jess when we first met. You know I'm not even that type of nigga, so she trying for nothing. My baby at home waiting for me, and she is all the woman I need." He told me before Mo yelled that it was his turn again.

"Come here y'all. I picked up on some scandalous shit, and I need to you to do something Jas to prove I'm right." I tried to talk low. The music was blasting, and it was hard to hear, but I didn't want to yell. I told them what happened, pointed to the chic, and came up with a plan. I walked over to the bar to act like I was ordering a drink while Candace and Jas watched from a distance.

"Can I get two Coronas with lemons in them?" Candace and Jas walked over just in time, as the girl walked back to her seats.

"Hey, I'm Alicia. I noticed you were looking at my brother over there. What's up, are you interested in him, or what?" I asked her, while Candace picked her beer up off the counter and stood to see what she would say.

"The one with the black thermal is your brother? He is sexy as hell. I saw him in here before, but we didn't get a chance to speak. Can you give him my phone number and tell him to hit me up. I know how to keep a secret if he do." She said, passing the napkin with her number on it.

"You got it. I'm going to hand it to him later when he's done. I don't want to interrupt him in the middle of his game." I took the napkin and walked back over to Candace and Jasmine.

"Bitch, she work with Jess and Mike. She told me she was here when they first met, so she is very aware that he is taken. She can keep a secret if he can. I'm telling you, these tricks nowadays don't mind being sidepieces. It's like sidepieces are the new fad. I feel like Lil' Kim when she said, "Get your own shit, why you riding mine?"

"Are you going to tell Mike? You know he ain't going to care, because he is all into Jess, but I think he should know to watch out for her. That shit sound like a setup. Oh shit, are you going to tell Jessica?" Jasmine asked me, and I wasn't sure how to answer it, but Candace did.

"Hell no. Not yet. She's probably going to cry, anyway. You know she ain't no fighter." Candace laughed, as she was saying it.

"Girl, you know you ain't right. Let's take some pictures with Mike and post them on IG so she knows that he is here with us. She should know by now ain't nobody fucking with our clique." We snapped pictures all night with the guys and watched this girl, basically, stalk Mike the whole time.

"Yo, I need y'all to do me a favor." Mike asked when he called all of us over.

"What's up?" I was the first to ask, because he knew that, if it was something foul, I was all for it.

"Y'all know I'm really feeling Jessica, and today, we were at my mom's house when she got a phone call saying she was pregnant. Now she talking about getting an abortion because she scared that the baby may have Down Syndrome, or some type of disability. I told her that I didn't care and that I didn't want her to kill my baby, but I would support her in her choice. Can you go over there tomorrow and talk to her, without being mean Alicia?"

"Well, I'm happy we can be pregnant together. Do she know how far she is yet?" Jasmine asked him.

"No, the first appointment is next week. I'm going with her, and I told her that she better make a decision quick, because if I hear the heartbeat, that's a wrap for an abortion."

"Man, that girl is not getting rid of that baby. She is in love with you, so stop worrying about that shit." Candace said, as we all watched a smile creep over Mike's lips.

"Bitch, you just talk too much. She didn't want to tell him. You know I can't with you. Darrell how do you deal with my sister?"

"Of course, we'll go after we get off work tomorrow, but listen here, playa. That chic gave me her number to give you, and she said she wouldn't tell if you don't. I don't trust her." But I'm giving you a heads up. I'm not telling Jess, because I know you're not like that, but be careful. Bitches that thirsty always have an agenda."

We watched Mike take the last swig of his beer, give dap to the guys, and head to his car. As he walked out of the door, I noticed that chic go out behind him, so we walked out right behind her. When we walked out, she turned around to go back like she wasn't following him. We stayed out and smoked a blunt in the parking lot, while Jasmine stood outside the car talking shit, because she couldn't.

It was a late September, so it wasn't too cold out. The guys walked outside, where we were, and Cornell yelled at me for smoking after only being out a week. He said that I wasn't giving my body time to heal and that he needed me to be strong for our plot against his brother. I know it was fucked up, him plotting against his brother, but fuck it; he tried to kill his wife, so hatred was all Cornell had towards him now.

Mike

I sat in my car and sent Jess a text before I started driving. I lit my blunt and waited, because if she was asleep, I didn't want to wake her by knocking.

Me: Hey baby, I'm on my way. Did you leave the key in the mailbox for me?"

Jess: You know I did. I told you I had a surprise for you, now come get it before I go to sleep.

Me: Bet, I'll be right there.

I sped out of the bar's parking lot when she sent me that text. I knew that chic followed me out, but I didn't turn around and acknowledge her, because then she would ask if I had her number. I know I should've told her that I wasn't interested, but fuck it, she'll get the hint when I don't call her. I turned the lights off, turned my alarm on, and grabbed the key out of Jess's mailbox. I noticed that all of the lights were off, as I locked the door, walked up the steps, and into the living room.

"Yo', Jess where you at?" I whispered, trying not to wake the baby but still looking for her.

She walked out of the room in this short, black, maid outfit, that she only had the bottom to; the suspenders covered her nipples, and she had on some black heels, and a feather duster.

"Excuse me, can I help you? Do you have a room on this floor?" She asked, standing there looking sexy as fuck. I guess we were roll playing, and I was so with this shit.

"Yes, my room is right there. I believe you just walked out of it. It looks to be squeaky clean, but you left the light off, and I can't see to turn it on." I said, playing along with her.

"I'm so sorry, sir. Please forgive me. I will turn it on." She said, bending over, showing me that she had no panties on. When she turned the light on, the room lit up red from the bulb. She had her handcuffs hanging off the side and she put stars on the ceiling. A canopy cover draped over top of the bed, and there was some flavored massage oil laid out.

"Thank you for doing a great job with my room. Is there anything I can do for you, because I don't have any singles for a tip?

"I would love to give you a massage if you don't mind, but if you have a girlfriend, we don't have to do anything." She said, still roll playing.

"Ok, I'm going to take a quick shower, if you don't mind. I will be right out, and you can give me that massage." I do have a girlfriend, but she doesn't know I'm here. When I walked back in, she was sitting on the bed with her legs crossed and laying on her elbows waiting for me.

"Ok miss, you can do my massage now." I said, dropping my towel and watching Jess lick her lips. She got on top of my back, poured the oil in her hands, and started working my shoulders, then my sides, back, legs and even my feet.

She told me to turn over, as she rubbed the oil all over my chest and stomach and moved down to my dick. I just laid there with my hands behind my head watching her. She went up and down with her hands still full of oil waking him up. She took the head in her mouth and spit on the tip before she started working her magic going up and down. I grabbed the back of her hair and started making love to her face. I loved having sex with her, and there was no need for me to look anywhere else.

"Oh shit, Jess. I'm about to cum. Don't stop. Aaaaah, damn baby. That shit was the bomb." I told her, as I watched her still sucking up every drop of cum I had. She stayed on her knees and crawled up to me, letting the suspenders drop off her shoulders. We kissed like our tongues were stuck together, as I felt her wetness dripping on my stomach. I turned her over to fuck her in those heels.

"Hey daddy, I want you to fuck me. No love making." She said, driving me wild, as I lifted her legs up and rammed my dick in her wet pussy. She screamed out and dug her nails in my back, but that's what she wanted.

"Yea, Daddy. Give Mami what she been waiting all day for. Fuck me. Yea, just like that. Oh yea. This is your pussy now. Show me you deserve it." She was yelling out, making me fuck her harder.

"Yes, baby, I want you to fuck me from the back just as rough." She told me, and I gave her what she wanted. "Oh shit, baby. I'm cumming. Don't stop. I need this right now." She said, now sitting up to kiss me, as I was hitting it. She started playing with her pussy and put her other arm around my head. I grabbed a handful of hair, as I beat that pussy up from the back, watching it squirt all over my dick.

"Shit, I'm cumin too. Aaaahhhhh, shit," we yelled out at the same time. She took the rest of the outfit off and laid back with her legs open.

"Now, Daddy, come have your dessert." I licked my lips and dove right in her pussy like it was ice cream, licking and sucking every bit of it down to the cone.

"Yea, baby. This is your pussy, and she wants you to taste all of her warm juices that she is about to send you. Suck that shit, baby. Oh my God, here I cum, here I cum. Ohhhhhh Mikkkeeee, God, I love you so much."

She must've screamed out by accident, because she laid there quiet once she rode that orgasm. I moved her over, so that I could lay behind her, and she took my arm, placed it on her stomach, and rolled over to tell me that she was keeping the baby. I can't lie, I was excited about the baby and nervous to tell her the same three words she just screamed out. I laid there with her in my arms, as so many thoughts clouded my mind. Then, I watched her sleep before I dozed off not too long after her.

I got up the next day around 9:30, and Jess was already out to work for the day. I was still contemplating what to do after she told me she loved me. I sent her a text.

Me: Good morning, I just got up. I'm going to run to my house, and straighten up, but I'll be by later if that's ok with you. I miss you already.

Jess: Mmmmm… you know what I miss already. I made you your own key, so you don't have to keep checking the mailbox. I left it on the kitchen counter, but it has a set of the truck keys on it, too, just in case, you need to use it or if I lose mines.

Me: Let me find out you using me for my dick and mouth. And, of course, I want the house keys. I was just waiting for you to decide when you wanted to come up off of them. I think I should have the keys to wear my family lives, don't you think?

Jess: Yes, baby, I do. Oh, one other thing, I'm not ashamed about what I screamed out. I do love you, but I also don't want you to feel the need to say it back unless you mean it. I won't hold it against you, because I'm still going to be with you.

Me: We'll talk about that later. Get back to work. And think about daddy all day, and know I'll be waiting to give it to you when you get home, if you need it.

Jess: Now, how can I focus on work with you talking like that? Have a good day, and be safe baby. I love you.

Damn, that girl is going to have me telling her I love her by the end of the day if I'm not careful. Shit, the last girl I said that to played me so bad that I didn't think that I could handle that again. I guess you have to take chances at some point in life, but I swear, if she does me wrong, I'll snap her fucking neck. I locked up the house and walked into her mom, walking in the house from food shopping.

"Hey, let me help you." I said, grabbing bags from the car.

"Mike, I just want to say that I love you for my daughter, and I know she is in love with you. I don't know if she told you yet, but she is keeping the baby, and I couldn't be happier for you two. I just want you to know when that stupid doctor hurt her that she vowed to never love another, but then you came. I think you captured her heart before she knew how to guard it from you. I want you to keep her safe, and I know you would never intentionally hurt her, but sometimes things happen. If you're not ready to be with her like she is with you, then if you leave now, it won't be as bad." She said, putting the food away.

"I'm not going anywhere, Ms. Gomez, and she is stuck with me for life now, whether she likes it, or not, so don't worry; she will always be safe with me, and I won't let any harm come to her." I told her, kissing her on the cheek before walking out.

I unlocked the car, opened the door, lit my blunt, and called Mo.

"Yo', Mo, can you come to my house? I need to talk to you for a minute." I asked him through the Bluetooth on my truck.

"Yeah, I'll be there in a few." He said, as I drove to my house to change. When I pulled into my driveway, I couldn't believe this bitch had the nerve to be sitting on my damn porch.

Ty

I can't believe that I had to relocate back to Maryland because of that bitch, Jasmine. No, I'm not going to call her that, because that's the wife and mother of my children. She just doesn't know it, yet. I knew that nigga, Mo, had another agenda, when I first picked Jasmine up that night. Duh, that's it. All I have to do is prove to Jasmine that Mo ain't shit so that she will leave him and come back to me. I don't know what took me so long to realize that that's what I needed to do.

"Hey, baby. Who are you in here talking to?" Adrian asked, walking into the room with a breakfast tray. I don't know how I keep ending up back with her when she is not who I want to be with.

"I'm not talking to anyone. I was just saying my thoughts out loud. Now, come here and give me what I need." I told her, pushing her to the ground.

"You got it. Anything you want, you know that." Adrian told me, before she gave me some great speaker performance.

After she left, I went into my home office to finish working on shit to destroy all those motherfuckers. The first on my list was Mike, Mo's brother. I saw that that nigga had just found him a new chic, and he seemed to be falling for her hard. I also knew that he had an ex, Maria that claimed to have a baby by him but left for whatever reasons. I'd been messaging her every day under a fake name, telling her that I'm Mike's friend. I told her that he missed her, wanted her to come back, and that he tried to replace her with someone new, but it wasn't working, because he still wanted her.

What do you know, she missed him something horribly, so she said, and couldn't wait to get back, but she didn't have the money. So, of course, I sent her a ticket and gave her a little extra money to get around when she got off the plane. I couldn't wait to sit back and watch how that whole relationship was about to crumble. She was adamant, too, about winning him back, and from what I hear, the new chic ain't about that life, so it was going to be fun to watch. That was what his ass got for jumping me at the fucking hospital; punk ass nigga. It was great being a lawyer and having good friends in high places. You could get all the information you need with no problem.

When I was done with him, I was moving on to Darrell. I was going to send people over to audit his books and setup surveillance on the shop. I remembered when his dumb ass was talking about all the different cops, mayors, teachers, and so forth, placing bets with him. Illegal gambling is a crime, my brother, and you're going down. Cornell already received his pain when I shot that bitch ass wife of his, Alicia. Too bad I only got her on the side. I tried to kill that bitch for that disrespectful spitting shit and for turning my brother against me.

But hey, I may throw some more drama their way just for the hell of it. I couldn't wait to let my mom know. She fucking moved back with my father, but that was only because he didn't want to die alone, with his cancer having ass. He couldn't stand my mother; the sight of her repulsed him, but he needed help right now, so he was using her. And Mo, Mo, Mo, and Mo, I saved the best for last. That nigga stole my girl, made me rape, beat and violate her, and he was going to pay for all that with his life, and that was a promise that I intended on keeping.

Whew! Shit, my dick was getting hard just thinking about how all this shit was going to fall into place. I walked over to the mini bar that I had installed in my office and poured me a shot of Jack Daniels. I opened up my computer, and Jasmine was my screensaver. That woman was beautiful, and I was going to get her back, especially with Mo out of the picture. I laid back, unbuttoned my pants, put my hands in my boxers, and rubbed my dick until he got hard. I took myself back to when Jasmine was on top riding my dick and when her juices were flowing all down my dick. Remembering how good her pussy was, had me busting all over.

I showered and logged back onto Facebook to see if Maria made it to the plane. I needed to start all kinds of fires, so when I go for Mo, he wouldn't see it coming. She added her destination at the airport with a caption saying, "Goodbye Texas; New Jersey are my roots and where the love of my life is waiting for me". I couldn't believe how dumb she was to come here without even speaking to Mike. I hoped that she spoke with her relative, because I was deleting her ass as my friend. I damn sure wasn't paying for her to stay nowhere. Shit, she lucky she got the ticket and a little extra. Now, let me get some shit together, so I can watch this shit unfold.

Mo

I just hung the phone up with Mike, who asked me to stop by his crib, which was unusual, unless something was up. That nigga barely at his shit, so if he asking somebody to go there, he must have really wanted to talk in private. I got up, jumped in the shower, got dressed, and headed downstairs. Ms. D always made breakfast for Jasmine and me, and anyone else that stayed over. Shit; she was Darrell's mom, but since that shit happened to Jasmine, she had been here, and it didn't look like she was going anywhere. That was good, though, because Jas would be exhausted once she had the baby, and I was sure that Ms. D would be big help.

"Good morning, Ms. D. Thanks for the breakfast, but I'm going to take mines to go. Mike hit me up, and I need to get to his house." I told her, grabbing two pieces of bread to make a bacon and egg sandwich.

"Let me holla at you real quick first." She said, in a stern voice like something was wrong.

"What's up?" I looked at her all crazy.

"I was at your mom's house when Mike brought Jessica over there, and it didn't go so well. I mean, you know how your mom is when it comes to who you boys deal with. Well, she was extra nasty to her, as if that child did something to her." She said, smoking her cigarette.

"What do you mean when you say extra nasty?" I quizzed her trying to find out what all happened.

"All Jessica said was hi and that she did work at the hospital with your mom. Then, you know Carol. She started going in on the girl about having a baby by a doctor and was talking about how she had better not start any shit between him and Mike. Then, after we found out that she was pregnant, she started asking Mike if the baby was his and if he was sure. I don't know what it is, but your mother is up to something; I can't put my finger on it. I want you to call or go see her, because as much of a bitch as she is, I know something ain't right." She replied, now putting the cigarette out.

"What the hell man? I'm about to call her when I get in the car. Shit, she tried it with Jasmine, but you know how my girl can get. Jas wasn't having that shit, and I didn't stop her. I mean, she wasn't disrespectful, but she got her point across to my mom, and that was the last of it. I'm on it, though. Thanks." I said, kissing her on the cheek and walking to my car. I dialed Jas' number and waited for her to pick up first.

"Hey, Baby. I was just thinking about you. What's up? You miss me already?" She asked, making me smile.

"Of course, I miss you. What kind of question is that? Anyway, Mike called and I'm on my way to his house, but Ms. D just told me some disturbing shit about my mom." I said, telling her what my mom did, and she couldn't believe it.

"We are supposed to be stopping by there when we get off, so I'll find out. That's fucked up baby. If that's what happened. I hope Mike had her back, because I know she won't say anything. We have to get her out more, because this scary shit ain't working for her. She is going to have to put her foot down at some point, don't you think?" She replied, waiting for me to answer.

"Yea, but she will know when the time is right to do that. Y'all can't make her do it if she doesn't want to. It's going to take something rough to happen for her to say something, but I will call you when I'm done finding out all that happened at Mike's. I love you." I said, before hanging up.

"I love you, too, baby." Jas copied into the phone. I dialed my mom's number and waited for her to answer.

"Hey big head. What are you doing?"

"Nothing, just getting off work and going home to clean the house up for my surprise."

"What surprise?" I wanted to know what she had up her sleeve too.

"Oh, nothing. You'll find out soon enough. What are you doing?"

"I'm on my way down to Mike's house. He called a little while ago, and I'm headed there right now."

"Yo', Ma. What happened when Mike brought his new girlfriend over there?" I asked her to see if she was going to tell me the truth.

"I don't like her. She works with me, and when that shit happened with her and that damn doctor, she acted as if it was everybody's fault. I would speak to her, and she would roll her eyes. You know I don't play that shit. And now Mike done went and got her dumb ass pregnant. How do we even know if the baby is really his? I swear, if my grandbaby is disabled, I'm whooping her ass." I was so disgusted by what she said that I almost hung the phone up on her ass.

"Ma, are you serious. I'm going to act as if you didn't just say that last remark. First off, that would still be your grandbaby, my niece or nephew, and you know it. That woman may have rolled her eyes at you, because she was going through something and didn't want anyone in her business. Yes, it may have been wrong, but Ma, you mean as hell to people all the damn time. I still can't believe you just said that shit. I hope you never say that shit to him, because he probably would never speak to you again. I'm telling you that because I love you, but that's his woman and their child." I told her, hoping that she would take back that statement.

"Oh well, that's how I feel. Anyway, I'm pulling up at home now, and I'll call you when my surprise comes. Love you," I really needed to smoke after that fucking conversation. I thought about what my mother said the whole fucking way, debating on if I was telling Mike. Hell no, I ain't saying shit. That was my brother, but that was hurtful. Now, I know how my mom feels about a disabled grandchild.

I pulled up in front of Mike's house and noticed that that wasn't Jessica's car. I grabbed the handle to my car, when Jessica pulled up behind me. She got out wearing a one-piece dress and some fuck me heels, so I knew what the hell that meant. She gave me a hug and asked,

"Hey, Mo, how long are you staying, and whose car is this?" She said, examining the car.

"Hey, Jess, I have no idea whose car this is, and by the looks of what you have on, I'm only staying a few minutes." I said, laughing, when she punched me in the arm.

"Really, don't be blowing my spot up like that. When's that last time you talked to him."

"I think it was about an hour ago. Why, what's up?"

"Oh, no reason. I called him twice and text him a few times, and he didn't answer. I talked to him this morning, and after our conversation, I decided to leave early and surprise him." She said, smiling.

"Oh, I think he's going to be surprised." I laughed, as we walked to the door, but I wasn't expecting what happened next. Jasmine called my phone, as Jess knocked on Mike's door, but no one answered. She looked at me, as if I knew why. She went to knock again, when someone answered Mike's door.

Jessica

I called Mike's phone twice and text him to see if he would bring me up something for lunch because I forgot to make it this morning. When he didn't answer, I figured that he was asleep since he said he was taking a nap. I told my boss that I was leaving early today, since I had so many sick days. I just used one for the rest of the day. I went home, showered, changed into a dress, and put on the heels that we fucked in last night. I asked my mom to pick Damien up from daycare, because I wanted to lay up with Mike all day, and I knew that it would be late when I got in.

I thank God for my mom every day. I mean, she has been my rock through my entire life, and I don't know what I would do without her. She helps me so much with Damien and gives me a break when I need one.

When Damien was still in my stomach, they told me that he was a healthy, normal baby. That all changed when he came out with Down Syndrome. The doctors said that there must've been a mistake with the test, but it didn't matter, because when I looked into his eyes, I fell in love instantly. He had his upward slanted eyes, small ears, and huge tongue that he stuck out a lot after crying. I loved everything about him, and I made a promise, at that very moment, that no one would ever hurt him because of his disability. He was such a happy baby, but he had his days when he didn't listen, and I didn't know if that was because he was about to turn two or not.

When I went to knock on the door, Mo's phone started ringing, and it was Jasmine. She told him to tell me hi and that they would be over later. I knocked on Mike's door, and no one came, which made my heart start beating fast. I looked back at Mo, who shrugged his shoulders, as if he didn't know why he wasn't answering either. I put my hand up to knock again, when some chic opened the door in one of Mike's robes.

"Hello, how can I help you? Oh, hey Mo, what's up?" I heard Jasmine yelling on the phone, asking Mo whose voice that was. I looked at Mo like he had two heads, when she spoke to him. I know, damn well, he didn't know Mike was fucking around and let me knock on this door.

"I'm Jessica. Mike's girlfriend. Is he here?" I asked, before she moved out of the way to let me in. Mo told Jasmine that he would call her back and hung the phone up. I walked past to get to Mike's bedroom and noticed that he had just stepped out of the shower, because his door was slightly opened. My heart dropped at the sight of him getting dressed, as if they had just finished having sex. Mo came behind me, pushing the door open, showing me the unmade bed, and his clothes on the floor, making matters worse.

I made sure that Mike looked into my eyes to see all of the hurt that he had just instilled upon me, before I walked back to the front, snatched my keys, and the ones I gave him earlier. I told her she could have him and jumped in my car. I started the truck, laid my head on the steering wheel, and cried until I noticed him coming to run out the house to the truck. I put the car in drive and tried to pull off, as he kept banging on the window for me to roll it down.

"Please get out of the way, Mike." I said, wiping the snot from my nose and the tears that came rushing down.

"No, I'm not moving until you let me explain. It's not what it looked like." He replied, looking like a deer caught in headlights.

"Oh really, because it looks like she answered the door wearing the robe that I had on the other day when I was here. Your bed is messy, and you just got out of the shower. Now, you tell me what the fuck am I supposed to think happened in there, or are my eyes deceiving me?" I cried to him, as the woman walked to the front door still in his robe, smiling.

"Jess, get out the car so that I can talk to you?" He yelled, trying to get the truck door open that I locked when I saw him running to the car. I almost opened the door when I thought I saw his eyes misting up, until that bitch screamed out to him,

"Come on, babe. I'm home, and you don't need her. I'm all the woman you need." I couldn't believe that she had basically just told me that they were together.

"Yo', shut the fuck up Maria. We are not fucking together. I don't even know why you're still here." He yelled back at her. She got up and walked into the house, while Mo just sat on the porch shaking his head smoking.

"I'm leaving the truck at Jasmine's house with the keys. I can't do this Mike. This right here that we had is over. You promised me that you wouldn't hurt me, and you lied. I love you so much that, just saying this, is killing me."

"I'm getting in the car to talk to you. Unlock the door." I unlocked the door so that he could hear it, but when he walked around the car, I pulled off. You could hear the tires screech, as I turned around the corner. I dialed up Alicia's number, because I knew that she would know what to do with her mean ass. When she answered, I just broke down crying and asked her could she meet me at Jasmine's house.

When I got to Jasmine's house, I noticed all three of them standing on the porch waiting for me to pull up. I took my stuff out the truck and walked over to them crying, when they pulled me in for a hug.

"Let's jump in Alicia's car. She is the only one that don't have a GPS on it." Candace said, taking the keys that I to handed her. She put them in the house and told Ms. D to tell Mike that he could pick them up there. Alicia started her truck, pulled off, and asked me what happened. She wanted detail for detail. I started telling her the story all the way up until when Mike said that woman's name, when she stopped the car making us all jerk.

"What the fuck, Licia?" Candace asked her, mad, because she hit her head on the dashboard. She looked back at me.

46

"Did you say he called her Maria?" She asked me, looking evil as hell. Shit, I was scared as hell to answer myself.

"Yea, he yelled some shit like, "I don't even know what you're doing here, Maria, before I pulled off."

"And you said she was in his robe? I mean, what the fuck was Mike thinking? I'm calling his ass on the phone." The phone was on the Bluetooth, so I could hear everything that was about to be said. Jasmine pulled me close, rubbing my back, and I appreciated that, because I had no friends. The phone started ringing before he answered.

"Yo', where the fuck is Jess at? I know she with your ass, because we at Jas' house, and Ms. D said that she left with y'all. I swear, Licia, if you don't put her on the phone, we are going to have a problem." He yelled into the phone. The girls looked at me, and I shook my head no, not wanting to talk to him.

"Mike, you know I love you. You are on speakerphone, but she said she doesn't want to speak to you. What the fuck happened over there, and why didn't you tell me that Maria was in town? You know I owe her an ass whooping." Alicia yelled into the phone.

"Jess, I'm sorry. I can honestly say that that wasn't what it looked like. Fuck this! Alicia, where y'all at? I'm not doing this shit over the phone." He yelled again in the phone. I didn't want any parts of Mike.

"Mike, I will always love you, but this is too much for me. I think it's best to end this now before I fall deeper and can't

47

get out. Everything you told me was a lie, and now, you can't be trusted. Forget about me, and go back to Maria." I reached and hit the end button on the steering wheel, as he was trying to speak. The phone rang back, and it was Mike.

"Alicia, I swear to God, you better tell me where y'all are right fucking now." He was now so heated that you could tell he was spitting.

"Bye, Mike." I pressed the end button again.

Mike

I couldn't believe that that bitch came to my house after all this time, and she didn't have Devon with her, so what the fuck was she there for? I didn't feel like dealing with any shit from her, I swear, I didn't. I hoped that Mo ass got there quick, because I may kill that bitch. I stepped out of the car, turned on the alarm, and walked up to my porch.

"What the fuck you want Maria? And, where is Devon?" I asked, walking past her to my house. She stood up and walked in behind me. I should've made her ass stand at the door, but I knew, damn well, she wasn't staying long.

"Is that anyway to treat your baby's mom." She had the fucking nerve to say, and with a straight face, I might add.

"What do you want for real Maria? I'm only here to change my clothes, and then, I'm out. I told her, dropping my keys on the counter and smiling when I noticed Jess's keys next to mines. That was my new boo, and I wasn't about to let Maria fuck it up, so she had to go.

"Mike, come sit in here with me, so I can talk to you, please." She said, patting the seat next to her. I opted out and sat on the loveseat across from her instead. Maria was Spanish, with a size six body, fresh Pedi and Mani, and hair hanging down her back. She was wearing a black halter dress and was looking as good as she did when she left. She licked her lips, looking at me, and I just looked down on my phone so that she didn't see me smirk.

"What you want?" I asked, again, because it felt like it was getting hot in the room.

"I want to come back home. I know I fucked up and just left you with Devon. I was young and dumb, chasing behind some nigga that ended up doing him when we got to Texas. He didn't want any part of Devon, because even though he is his, you and I were together, and he was basically yours. He is willing to pay child support and allow you to adopt him if you want. I really want us to be a family. We can have more babies, the wedding we used to talk about, all that." She said, now standing over me, naked, as I looked up to speak. My dick stood at attention right away, but I couldn't do that to Jess, no matter how hard I was.

"Look, it's been two years, and I may have thought about it if this was six months ago, but I'm with someone else now, and she's all I need and want right now. She is having my baby, and I'm going to try to make it work with her. I'm sorry, but I can't just leave her, because you decided to realize what you had.

I want to see Devon, and we can start up the adoption papers tomorrow. Even though you've been away, I've watched him grow, and he is still my son, so get dressed, because this right here ain't happening tonight or ever again." I told her, walking to where my room was and shutting the door.

She started crying, but I just ignored her and got my ass in the shower. I thought I heard someone knock at the door, but Mo wasn't coming for a while, so I knew it wasn't him. I kept thinking about Jess the entire time that I was in the shower and couldn't wait to get back to tell her my feelings were the same. I stepped out and noticed my door was cracked, as I started getting dressed and had no idea Jess was standing there watching me. Fear took over my body, as I remembered that I left Maria standing there naked, and she probably opened the door that way with her smart ass. I saw all the hurt in Jess's eyes, and I couldn't get dressed fast enough to stop her from leaving.

Mo just stood there shaking his head, when I heard Jess yell to Maria that she could have me. I was crushed that she gave me away after what we shared and after she told me she loved me. I felt my eyes becoming misty, as I tried to get her to stop from leaving, when that dumb bitch Maria started talking shit, causing Jess to pull off.

I ran into the house, threw Maria her clothes, and kicked her the fuck out, while Mo and I jumped in his truck to get to Jasmine's. I knew that that was where she was going, but I was too late; they had already left, and she refused to speak to me on the phone. I went to her job the next day, and she asked to be moved to the ICU floor, where they wouldn't allow me in.

She wouldn't take any of my calls, but she did allow me to see Damien. I would send her a text, and she would drop him off to her mom's. I took him over to Candace's house a few times to play with the kids. They were so overprotective of him, because he was so small, and they knew he was different. Jess would've loved to see that in person, but I sent her pictures and videos. I knew that she saw them, because she left the read on her text messages so that I would know that she got all of my messages. I hadn't seen Jess in three weeks, and my heart was aching so bad. I called up Alicia, because I knew that they spoke every day now, and I wanted to know how she was really doing.

"Hey, Lee Lee. What's up? I just wanted to know how Jess was doing?" I called her the nickname we gave her. She knew I wanted something when I called her that.

"What you want me to do? And Jess is fine. I think she is finally getting over your ass... Sike." She said, when she noticed how quiet I got.

"Lee Lee, I know y'all asses going to Lamont's party. Can you bring her with you please? I really need to see her."

"Damn, nigga it sound like your ass is sprung. Ha, ha, she must got that fire shit like us. Whew! You picked a good one. Now we know she really one of us." She said, puffing in the phone, and I could tell that she was smoking. She had been smoking too much since she got shot, and I was going to have to hit her up later about that, but right now, Jess was my main focus.

"Ok, but your ass owe me an ounce of trees, and I'm not playing." She told me.

"I know you fucking weed head." I laughed in the phone.

"She was coming anyway. We been out shopping all day, but she doesn't know you're going to be there, so don't fuck it up."

I smiled when she told me that and went into my closet to pick out something to wear. Shit, I had so much new stuff but didn't go out as much anymore, so I decided to wear a cream, Sean John sweater and some black jeans with some cream Timbs. I put my necklace on, two diamond earrings in each ear, my class ring on my finger, and my Armani Cologne on that she loved smelling on me. It was 10:15 when I walked out the door to pick up Mo, Darrell, and Cornell.

We been with Cornell almost every day and even started treating him like he been around forever. We found a parking spot and walked in the club after being checked. I noticed that my sisters weren't there, which meant neither was Jess. We walked over to the VIP section, dapped it up with our boys, and started ordering drinks.

The song "Ascensions" by Maxwell was spinning when I saw the girls walk in, but I didn't see Jess yet until some guy stepped from in front of her. She was breathtaking with her hair freshly cut into a shorter bob like Halle Berry's. She had on a white shirt dress barely covering her ass; with the front hanging down almost showing her chest, and slits on the sleeves, with some over the thigh boots, hoop earrings, light makeup, and her cell in her hand. I saw them find a seat in a booth and enjoy the music waiting for their drinks.

Alicia: Hey, Mike, she here. What do you think?

Me: I'm going to fuck you up bringing her out dressed like that. But she is beautiful. Thank you.

Alicia: I love you too bro. Now you better do right by her tonight. I don't know if I can make it happen twice.

Me: I got you.

After Alicia and I text, I sent a message to Jess.

Me: Damn, baby, you look gorgeous. I miss looking at your pretty face every day.

I watched her look down at her phone, smile, then look around for me. I asked Lamont could he go ask the DJ to play a song for me, since it was a party. It was only right to play our song. I sat back with my arms up on the seat watching Jess as the DJ said, "This song goes out to Jess from Mike."

Jessica

The girls had shown me so much love in the last three weeks being away from Mike and all. They told me that I was their sister, now, and that, even if we didn't get back together, they would still be around and make any other chic he messed with, life's miserable. They were so funny though when we went shopping today. They were taking me to some 90's party for one of their high school friends, and I was happy because I needed to get out.

I had been dodging Mike every which way possible, because I knew that he would come up with all these different excuses, and I didn't have the strength to hear them. They told me that he broke his phone when I wouldn't talk to him, but oh well. I got dressed over Jasmine's house and ran right into Mo, as I got there.

"How long are you going to make my brother suffer?" He asked me, when I walked up to the house.

"He's not suffering. He has Maria, and if he didn't want her, then she shouldn't have been there. He hurt me bad, Mo, and I don't know if I can excuse that." I ran upstairs, because I was running late, and they wanted to do a makeover on my ass, as they say. When they were finished, I was shocked; I didn't even look like myself.

"If Mike saw me in this short ass dress he would kill me." I told them, admiring myself in the mirror.

The girls looked at me and said at the same time, "Girl, fuck Mike, but if you want to make him sweat, this is the way to do it. He will be pissed when or if he sees you, but fuck it. It's his loss and the next man's gain, right?" Candace said.

"I don't know, y'all. I'm still not over Mike. Maybe this isn't a good idea." I told them, sitting on the bed, now feeling myself getting upset.

"Girl, let's go before you sour the mood for everybody." Alicia said.

When we walked into the club, it was packed, and I could barely see, which makes me nervous as hell. Too many people in one place at a time was a recipe for disaster. I was in there looking for the exits before we even sat down. Some guy stopped me as soon as I walked in asking if he could buy me a drink, but I had to pass, being pregnant and all. I still smoked a little weed here and there, though, to keep me calm.

We found a booth and sat down when I got a text from Mike telling me how beautiful I looked. I looked around but couldn't find him anywhere; I knew he was watching me. The DJ came on the microphone saying Mike requested two songs for us, but I didn't know what it was until it started. It was our song when we first met but the remix.

Come and talk to me,
I really want to meet you girl,

I really want to know your name,
Oh, come and talk to me.

"Oh shit, bitch, bye." Jasmine said. When I looked up, Mike was standing there holding his hand out. Damn, this nigga was beyond fine standing in front of me. I let him walk me out to the dance floor and spin me around in front of everyone. He grabbed me close with our bodies grinding and whispered in my ear.

"Baby, I'm so sorry. I can't sleep or eat without you in my life. I need you so bad. Can you please forgive me?" I looked up, and he lifted my chin kissing me passionately on the dance floor, and I let him. The next song came on, and I cried right there from the emotions the song brought me,

Sorry I left you,
Left you crying,
Since you've been gone,
I've been all alone.

"Baby, I'm not leaving you. You hurt me so bad, though. I needed time away to teach you a lesson. You are right here engraved in my heart, and I can't etch you out, but you better not hurt me, again, or I swear, I'm out. No matter how bad I hurt." I told him, letting him wipe the tears, with his fingers that left my eyes.

"How did you know what really happened?" He asked me, trying to figure out why I had a change of heart.

"My mom told me everything you told her, and she said she believed you, so I trust my mom intuition. Plus, the girls told me that that's not the type of man you are, and if you said nothing happened, then it didn't. Baby, let's just go. I missed you something terrible, and I need you back in my life, and you know where else." I said, smiling, grabbing his dick. Alicia walked up and told us to pose, as she took a picture, and I'm sure she posted it on IG. Mike grabbed my hand, when we walked right into Maria, who was there, probably, watching the whole thing.

"Hold on, baby." I said, turning around. "Yea, bitch, this right here belongs to me." I kept talking, as I pointed to Mike. "Don't you ever disrespect me like that again? See, that was the old Jess, but don't get it twisted. I will fuck you up if it happens again." I told her, before spitting in her face.

Mike grabbed me up. "Now, I know you been with my sisters too long, because you don't even act like that."

We drove back to Mike's house, and he helped me get out of the car and carried me into the house, like we were married. He locked the door, turned around to hand me the keys to his house, and said, "This is your house, too. Now, I want my keys back." I knew that he meant the ones to my house that I took back from him.

"Oh yeah, you have to earn those back. And since that's the case, I want a new truck. That other one had a fucked up memory, and I won't step foot back into it." I told him, watching him let out a chuckle and whisper that he was going to fuck his sisters up for turning me like them. I couldn't do anything but smile.

He took my hand, led me to the bedroom, sat me on the bed, and unzipped my boots. He kissed and sucked on my toes, and he had me moaning instantly. He ran his tongue up my leg straight to the middle, took his hands to remove my thong, and put his mouth directly on my throbbing clit. I missed him so much that I came almost as soon as he touched it. He put his fingers in my pussy, pulling them out to suck the juices off, then placing them back in, finding my g-spot. He was blowing and biting on my clit, and I started shaking, as I waited for him to suck my body dry. The orgasm overtook my body so much that it took me a few minutes to come down from that high. He just watched and waited patiently for me. He always let me get mines a few times before he got his. He took my dress off and climbed on top of me, rubbing the head of his penis up and down my lips, making my body quiver, as I waited in anticipation for him to enter me.

He entered my body taking his time. It was like he wanted to tell me something through his strokes instead of his voice.

"Aaaaaah shit, baby. It feels so good, and I missed you so much. Oh God, baby please don't hurt me like that again." I said, in between breaths from the slow, yet powerful strokes that he was giving me. I closed my eyes enjoying the feeling that he was giving my body.

"I'm not leaving you girl. I'm so sorry for hurting you, and no one will ever get this but you." He said, still taking his time, but making my heart melt from the things he was saying. "I love you so much girl, and I realized it even more when I thought I lost you over some bullshit." He said, stopping in mid-stroke, and when I opened my eyes, he had a few tears coming down his face. I couldn't believe he was crying, but deep down inside, I was happy.

"Baby, I'm not leaving you. I just wanted you to hurt like I was. I needed you to feel my pain and understand that I would." I told him, now wiping the few tears he had falling. I can't believe I broke him down and got him to fall in love with me. I thought it would be harder, because of how guarded he was, but I guess you can't help who you love.

"I know now that you are what I want, and I don't ever want you to think otherwise." He started making love to me over and over all night. I don't think we went to bed until five in the morning. I woke up to five text messages and eight missed calls from the girls. I didn't have any from my mom, because I text her when we left the club and told her I would be with Mike. She probably already knew I would be staying, because Damien was with his dad. I got up to use the bathroom around one in the afternoon, when Mike grabbed my arm.

"Baby, you leaving?" He asked, still half sleep.

"No, honey, I'm going to the bathroom, but check your phone. I got missed calls and texts from the girls telling me to call them.

"Mo and Darrell text him that after you spit in Maria's face, she and her friends were about to come after you when Alicia and Candace beat their ass. Mo was already on his way down when we were leaving, so he grabbed Jasmine before she got in it, being pregnant and all."

"Baby, I'm sorry. I didn't know they would end up fighting. I could've stayed and jumped in it. Not sure how much I would've done, but I would've helped."

"Girl, you weren't jumping in shit with my baby in there, but on a serious note, now that I gave you my heart, you better not play with it or step on it. I told you I love hard so you better really love a nigga." He said, kissing me and rubbing my stomach.

"Oh, I'm going to show you how much I really love this nigga right here." I said, pointing to him, before going down to give him what he loves.

"Oh shit, baby. Show daddy what he missed." He said, as I went to work on his prized possession. We made love all day until everybody got tired of calling and texting us and showed up to the house four cars deep, with the kids and all.

"I love how tight your family is."

"Bitch, please, we your family now too. Especially, since Mike told everybody on IG he loved you. He screenshot the picture Alicia took and put it on his page and captioned it. "*I love this woman, and I'm not ashamed to tell the world.*" I just looked up at him with misty eyes; I was so in love with him and I was happy that he told everyone he felt the same.

"I love you, baby."

"I love you, too, girl, and don't let no shit come in between us again." He said, turning me around to rub my belly from behind. I hadn't been this happy in a long time. The girls started telling me what happened after I left, and the guys ended up ordering food for everybody. It was after midnight when everybody left, and my body was exhausted. Mike and I just fell asleep under one another until his phone kept ringing non-stop around four-thirty in the morning. When he answered, I knew something was wrong.

"Alright yo, I'm on my way." He responded to the person on the phone. He hung the phone up and started getting dressed. He looked over at me to see if I was awake. "Baby, I have to go, but call me when you get up. I love you." He said ,waiting for me to respond.

"Ok, be safe, and I love you, too." He came back and sat on the bed to ask me.

"Are you going to ask me where I'm going?"

"No, I'm not. If you want me to know, you'll tell me. You always told me, the less I know, the better."

"That's my baby. I was just checking. Don't forget to call me when you get up." He said, before he walked out the door. I jumped out the bed and ran behind him trying to catch him before he left.

"Ugh, no bro. You take that truck. I'm taking yours. I told you, I wasn't driving that shit no more, and I meant it." I yelled out the door, when he came back to get the other keys, smacking me on the ass on the way back out.

I locked all the doors and got back in bed, when my phone rang from Candace asking if Mike left. When I told her yeah, we ended up calling Jasmine and Alicia on three-way to find out what happened. Alicia filled us in on what happened, but something was fishy about that entire shit. After we got off the phone, it was after six, and Mike still wasn't back. I got dressed, grabbed his keys, and headed out the door.

Ty

I sat back in my car from a distance watching this nigga let this chic go up in his house. I mean, shit. If I knew the chic was this bad, I would've tried to fuck her first. I watched Mike take his time getting out of the truck, probably wondering what she was doing there. They walked in the house, and shortly after, another bad Spanish chic got out of a car with punk ass Mo pulling up behind her. Those niggas really did look alike, besides that mole on his face.

"Now, this is the best part coming up." I spoke out loud to myself, as I watched her walk to the door. I'm going to move my car a little closer, but still out of sight so that I could hear what was about to happen.

I rolled my window down and saw the chic that had just pulled up with Mo come running out the door, crying, with that nigga Mike darting out behind her. She rolled the window down yelling at him, because he wouldn't let her go anywhere without letting him explain. She started screaming at him about Maria being inside with no clothes on and in some robe. I was getting a kick out of the whole situation, because word around town was this dude was in love, so to see this happening had me tickled. Just when I thought it couldn't get any better, ole girl started talking shit about how he didn't need her, kind of making it seem as if they were back together.

Mo took a seat on the porch shaking his head and lighting his blunt, as Mike walked back to the house, cursing her out for even opening her mouth. I knew this nigga was going to chase after her, so I followed them hoping to get a glance of my baby Jasmine, since she wouldn't see me. Unfortunately, we missed all of them, because the guys were standing outside, and Mike was leaned up against his truck arguing with someone. Whatever the other caller said pissed him off so bad that he threw his phone and cracked it in half, before punching the glass out in his truck.

Damn, that chic must have threw it on his ass for him to act like that. I'd always known him to be the quiet type. You know the kind that just sit backs and observes everything, but I guess good pussy would have you do crazy things. Well, that was good enough for me. I was going to head back to Maryland until my next plan comes to play.

It had to be three weeks before I got the call that they were about to raid Darrell's shop, and I wanted front row seats. I dropped everything and went back to Jersey in a rental so no one would recognize me. It was four in the morning, when I watched Darrell get out his car and run into the garage. My boy told me that they had a warrant, but where the fuck were they? This nigga is getting way too much time alone to destroy evidence. Just as I was thinking that, FBI agents, a local police car, and Cornell walked into the garage. Mo and Mike showed up around 4:30, I guess, to show their support.

"What the fuck was Cornell doing there? I know this nigga ain't helping him get out of this shit." I said, out loud to myself. Around 6:30, they walked Darrell out in handcuffs and put him in the back of the police car.

"Yes, another one bites the dust." I yelled in my car, pounding on the ceiling. Just as I was about to leave, my car door opened.

"What up fuck nigga?" Mike asked, as he jumped in the front seat rolling a blunt. "I know you set all this shit up, but it's ok, because your time is coming.

"What are you waiting for then? I mean, shit, you can just kill me here, right now." I asked him, sounding all cocky.

"Oh no, it's not time for you to die yet. See, I have plans for you. I mean, we have plans for you." He said, once Mo jumped in the back seat and put a gun to my temple.

"We know you been skipping in and out of town lately, and it's ok, because it hasn't affected anyone. See, everything you do, we will always be two steps ahead of you, so have a safe ride back to Maryland. We will see you soon." Mo said, as he shot me in the leg on his way out the car.

"Oh, shit, oh shit. I'm bleeding everywhere." I yelled out, as Mike took his time getting out.

"That's just a warning, but try to be waiting for us when we come for you. I would hate for you to be surprised. See you soon, fuck nigga."

"Can somebody help me?" I screamed in the car, trying not to move. I took my shirt off and tied it around my leg, hoping to stop the bleeding. I thought about driving to Maryland, but there was no way I could make it there without bleeding out. I put the local hospital in my GPS and drove to the emergency department.

"What do you know? Mike's bitch works here in the registration department. It must be my fucking lucky day." I walked in, and the nurses and doctors came running out to assist me. I looked in her direction, but she was looking down on her phone smiling.

I had to stay in the hospital for two days to let these motherfuckers observe me. I waited for missy to come back to work, but it wasn't until two days later that she returned. I waited patiently for her to get off and was walking to Mike's truck, when I followed behind her. I already knew where Mike lived, so I wanted to know where she was going, because it was close and not in the direction of Mike's house. She hopped out and used a key to open the door to a house. *Bingo.* "This is where she lives," I thought out loud to myself. I wrote down the address and drove back to Maryland. I knew that that information would come in handy.

Cornell

Ever since that shit with Ty shooting Alicia, I'd been having nightmares like that nigga was back in town. I hired a private investigator and had him followed, and sure enough, that nigga was dipping in and out of town to see my dad, and I wasn't sure why else. One day, I received a call from a friend of mines that worked at the FBI, and I was shocked to hear what he had to say.

"Cornell, long time no hear my brother." Calvin said. Calvin was a middle-aged white guy that was caught up in a drug raid gone bad. He and some of his other team members were conducting huge drug raids and turning over the drugs and guns, but keeping the money. One of the guys working with him got divorced from his wife, and she went to Internal Affairs, where they did an investigation. They were all charged, but gout out on bail, when he called me up begging me to take their case.

The reason I took it was because I was still new to the game, and I knew that that would boost my credibility. Needless to say, Ty had his cop friends destroyed evidence and tampered with some of the witnesses that were in jail. The case made national news and 15 witnesses, and four weeks of trial later, they were all acquitted and offered their positions back on the force. They always told us that they were forever in our debt, so when he called me up, I figured some shit popped off.

"Hey, Cal, man. How's it going? How's the family?" I asked him.

"Everybody's good. Listen, I need you to meet me downtown today around 4:30, no questions asked until you get there."

"Ok."

When I arrived, he was already sitting there with two of the other guys that I represented. Once all the hellos were finished, we ordered some drinks and began talking. He started telling me how Ty contacted him wanting to set up some dudes from Jersey that did him dirty. I just listened as he talked.

"He wants us to put surveillance on some garage that he claims that they do illegal gambling out of with politicians, among other respectable people. Now, me not talking to you, yet, I agreed, because of the work you guys did to get us off, but I was not into setting no niggas up, and then, I have to worry about my family. What I'm asking you is do you know these guys? And are they all that he say they are before I go to my boss and have him open up an investigation?"

"You know Ty has always been a hot head, thinking he was invincible. What happened was he met a woman from Jersey, fell in love with her, beat, raped and violated her in ways that you can't imagine. Of course, she wants no parts of him, but she won't go to the cops. Once I found out he did that to the woman, I disowned him, but not before he came into my house and shot my wife. He claimed that she was taking me away from him, because I knocked him out in the store for jumping bad with her. All I'm saying is everybody does their dirt, and if it ain't broke, don't fix it. But I believe this information is what I've been looking for along with what you gave me two months ago. That first lead, we are handling this weekend." I told him.

Three weeks later, I called Darrell up at four in the morning and told him that there was a search warrant and the locals and FEDs were going to his shop. I told him not to worry, and that I had his back, but I needed him to go there. When he got there, he called, and we put the plan in motion. The few guys that Ty and I knew from the FBI showed up, and one of the local cops that Darrell and I knew came as a decoy also. We walked in with Mo and Mike showing up not too long after to make all of it look real.

We sat in there for over an hour drinking and laughing, while watching my brother's dumb ass sitting out in the car on the camera installed outside the shop. We finished setting up everything we were going to do to get Ty. To make it look real, we had Darrell walked out in handcuffs with an FBI agent walking out, with four boxes of nothing. We had to make sure that the scene looked as real as possible, so that the other FBI agent wrapped caution tape around the building. The scene was the perfect set up for Ty, who was probably happy that they did that for him. He didn't notice Mike and Mo walking up to his car.

He was such a cocky nigga that he is going to get his own self killed, trying to play a bad guy with people who grew up doing that shit. When we got out of Ty's view, we let Darrell out and called Mo to pick him up. Alicia already knew what was going on, and I know that she and the girls were on the phone all morning talking about it. Alicia was my down ass chic, and I couldn't have asked for a better wife.

It was unfortunate that Ty made me choose between him and my wife. I would always love him, because he was my brother, but I couldn't save a nigga that didn't want to be saved. At this point in my life, after almost losing her, I know I made the right choice. That nigga told me I better be happy it wasn't me when he walked out. I knew that we had to hurry up and get rid of his ass before shit got real bad.

Darrell

I couldn't believe that nigga tried to set me up and get away with it. I was sitting in a room with my worst nightmare. The FEDS!!!! Thank goodness these were Cornell's boys, and I didn't have anything to worry about. We came up with a plan on how to make it all look real when we finally got up from drinking. My phone started ringing as I was sitting there.

"Hey baby, what's up?" I asked Candace, because I knew her nosy ass was going to call me once she talked to Alicia and found out what we were really doing.

"Nothing, I wanted to know if you wanted me to make you breakfast, or were y'all going to grab something?"

"Nah, I'm good, baby. I'll be home shortly, though. Make sure you're waiting for me naked when I get there." I whispered to her, as she purred into the phone letting me know that her kitty was ready to be pet. After I hung up the phone, I noticed that all my boys were looking down at their phones. I knew that the girls were calling or texting to check up on them, too. Shit, if one of us answers, they expected all of us too.

I just sat back in my chair listening to everyone bullshit, when I started thinking about how Mo and Mike became my brothers for life. We were about 15 years old, when we were at one of the basketball courts rolling dice. The game was getting serious with niggas losing money and ready to fight. Mo and Mike were always playboys, so they were standing against the fence talking to some hoes. The girls loved them, because they were twins and did everything together. Shit, those niggas even switched up on some girls; unless they recognized the mole, they had no idea which one they were with. These niggas were straight from the projects and knew better than to come out not strapped. Shit was always bound to pop off, especially at the courts.

We were so deep in the game that it was too late to run, when shots rang out in our direction. People were dropping right and left to hit the ground. Mo and Mike moved away from the girls and slowly dipped behind some cars, watching the car move slowly, still spraying. Mo walked up to the driver's side and let two off in his skull. When the passenger realized what had happened, Mike waited for him to get out, pointed his gun, and pulled the trigger, leaving them lying out in the street. Everybody heard about them, but people thought it was a myth about how bad they really were until they saw it firsthand. This was before cell phones were out, so no one recorded shit, and they knew not to speak about it.

I didn't really know them at the time but walked up to them and thanked them for looking out. I offered them some money, but they declined saying it was kids outside, and that that was why they retaliated. Weeks went by after that shooting occurred, and a hit was put out on the twins, because somebody opened their mouth. I still wanted to repay them for saving my life, so I inquired about who put the hit out. I walked up to them sitting at the park on the benches like they didn't have a care in the world.

"Yo', what's up, you want to hit this?" Mike asked, handing over the blunt. I took a pull and handed it back, then let them know who put the hit out on them. We dapped it up, as I walked away. Two days later, the snitch perished in a fire set by Mike. The person who put the hit out was killed in his sleep with a silencer, while his mom slept in the next room. The twins came back and thanked me for the information, and we vowed to have each other's back ever since. That was sixteen years ago.

We were at a football game, when I met Candace, who I'd been with now since my junior year, and she had a sister, Jasmine. They were mixed with black and white and resembled each other a little bit not as much. When Mo and Mike met Candace, they loved her, instantly, because she was gangsta and down for whatever. But when they met Jasmine, her and Mike hit it off, because they liked the same music, but Mo couldn't stand her. He thought she was stuck-up, had a nasty ass attitude, and was a bitch. She really wasn't into the street dudes, and I think Mo was feeling her back then, but she wasn't feeling the same. That was why it was funny as hell that they fell in love years later.

Over the years of being together, we have had politicians, cops, mayors, and other important people from our town and others, placing bets on a regular. We had made so much money off these people's addiction, that there was no need to still be in business, and with Cornell making our books look legit, we were good. Unfortunately, when it was time to pay, people thought it was a game until the twins started showing their true colors again. Nobody wanted to deal with them, so we didn't have any more problems.

"I believe all of our problems will go away when we get rid of Ty. It doesn't seem like anything happened until he came into the picture, so it's time to take that trip twins." I said, because that was what I called them when I spoke to both of them. They both nodded their heads and said that we would leave the following Sunday.

"She works Monday through Friday, and that will give us time to get down there, speak with her, do a little surveillance, and be back the following Sunday, before it hits the news." Mo said, standing up, looking at the camera and pointing out that Ty was still there.

"Alright, Cornell, can you lock the doors as we walk out?" I asked him.

"You got it, and thanks again guys for doing this for me. We won't speak of this to anyone, and if it did come up deny, deny, deny.

"We are good to go. Darrell, can you turn around so that I can place the cuffs on you?" Calvin asked, as I did what he asked and walked out with him.

Jasmine

I know this nigga better have his ass here by 9:30 so we can go to my doctor's appointment together. Shit, I could've went by myself, but he said he needed to attend each one so that he could hear everything that the doctor told me to and not to do. He was getting on my damn nerves with this pregnancy, and I was only four months… way past the first trimester. I threw on some pink yoga pants, a white t-shirt, and some white Air Force Ones that he just had gotten when we went shopping. He walked in the door yelling up the steps for me to hurry up like his ass didn't just get there.

"Hello to you, too. I was just getting ready to call you to see if I was riding solo." I yelled down the steps grabbing my cell and purse.

"Girl, let's go. You always talking shit, now, like I won't say anything back. Go get in the car, while I take a piss real quick."

He got in the car, kissed me on the lips, and started driving. When we got there, it was only a few cars in the parking lot, and I was happy, because that meant that it wasn't crowded. We walked in, went to the nurse's station to sign in, and waited for the nurse to call me to the back. We sat in the chairs watching the TV, when Mike and Jess walked out hand-in-hand.

"Bitch, you didn't tell anyone you had an appointment. We could've came together and left these sleepy ass niggas home."

"Mike wasn't supposed to come after he blew a gasket the first time we came, because the doctor came in with a male resident. I had to send his ass to the car acting like a damn baby throwing a tantrum and shit. When he called me, I told him where I was going, and his ass insisted. I didn't even plan on making this appointment until Laura called to tell me the doctor wanted to see me."

"Well, I want to go eat after this. Y'all feel like waiting, so we can go together?" I asked them, with Mo pushing me to the back.

"Yea, Mike said he hungry anyway, so we'll be out here."

I looked at the nurse, who was looking at my chart without lifting her head up. She finally looked up, because she had to start doing my vitals, when I realized that she was the same chic trying to fuck Mike some months back.

"Yo', I thought you worked at the hospital." I asked her, seeing her face turn red, because she was busted. The doctor walked in just as she was about to answer. He had me undress and completed the ultrasound. We got our 3-D picture of the baby, and I started to get dressed. The girl walked back in to give me my next appointment, so I asked her the same question.

"I thought you worked at the hospital." I quizzed her again.

"I do, but on my off days, I help out here."

Mo was sitting in the chair looking down on his phone not paying me any mind. I got up off the table nice and slow, fixing my clothes and walked to the counter area where she was.

"You are a trifling ass bitch. You that chic that was trying to fuck my brother Mike at the bar, and you friends with his girl. You know she ain't that type of girl to say anything, but I am, and I should beat your ass right here, bitch." I said, before I started raining blows to her face, causing Mo to jump up out of his chair.

"Yo', Jas, what the fuck?! Get off of her. You pregnant, and you up in here fighting. Get your shit! Let's go." He was dragging me out the room, as I started cursing that bitch out.

"I wish you would press charges on me. I'll come back and kill you myself. Ok, babe, I'm ready now."

When we got out the waiting area, I grabbed Jess by her hand and stormed out the doctor's office. Mike and Jess had no idea what happened, but I figured I'd tell her on the car ride to Perkins, because I knew that Mo didn't want to drive with me right now.

"What happened in there, Jas? Why did everybody go running back there? Mike was mad as hell that the door was locked and that he couldn't get to the back. If I didn't know any better, he was about to take his gun out and shoot the door down if y'all didn't come right out. Yes, I know he carries it, but I let him think I am naïve. I know a lot more than he tells me." She said, shocking the hell out of me.

"Well, that bitch Laura you call your friend tried to fuck Mike that night a while back when we went to the bar. She gave Alicia her number and told her to tell him that she wouldn't tell if he didn't. You know, some grimy bitch shit, and since you're not that kind of chic, I beat her ass for you. Girls like that need to be taught a lesson that not every man wants a side piece."

"I appreciate that Jas, but I wish you would've told me you were about to do that. I mean, I could've got some hits in myself. Of course, Mike would've killed me, but that's foul. I knew something was up with her, because the day she called and told me the results of my test, she said that I'd better keep him happy before someone else does. I just nixed it off, but I need to pay more attention. It doesn't matter now, because y'all are the only ones I hang around." Mike was just shaking his head, laughing, as he took Jess's hands into his.

"Oh, you're not going to hold my hand." I said to Mo, who tried to walk ahead of me like he was still mad.

"Jas, I swear that, if something happens to my baby, I'm going to kill your ass." He told me, with a face so scary that I knew not to pull no shit like that again.

"Oh baby, I'm sorry. Let's go back in the car, so I can make it up to you."

"Nope, your ass is on punishment from the D. Now, let's go eat." He said, leaving me standing there.

"Ok, then that means your ass don't talk to Katy either." I said, when he stopped dead in his tracks and turned around to walk back to me.

"Listen, that is my pussy, and I will talk to her when I feel like it. I dare you to try and keep her from me, and see who she gets mad at first." He said, making me laugh, because he was right. Even if he didn't give me the D, he still gave me mind-blowing orgasms off his head alone, and I refused to be without both. When we walked in, those two were already at the table waiting for us to come in.

"Y'all done punishing each other on who's going to hold out longer?" I just punched him in the arm laughing, because he knew us so well.

"Baby, they do this all the time. That's why I said let's just go." He told Jess, who put her head down like she was embarrassed. We started eating our food when Mike told Jess that he had to leave town for the week, which I already knew, because Mo was going, too. One never left town on a mission without the other.

"Ok baby, be safe. And remember, you need to hit me off before you go, so I don't stray while you're gone." She started laughing, but he didn't think shit was funny.

"Jess, don't play with me. You gonna have me murk somebody's ass when I get back." He told her, giving her that same look that Mo gave me. Damn, these niggas think alike and everything. I guess it was true what they say about twins being in touch with one another.

"Awww baby, don't be mad. You know this kitty only purrs for you." I don't know what the fuck she did to Mike, but that nigga was definitely in love.

"Come on, y'all, not in here. I'm trying to eat." We just bust out laughing and finished chilling, before leaving to go our separate ways.

"The day came for the guys to leave, and Mo still had me on punishment from the D, but he did speak to Katy, making her cum five times last night. Jess called me when Mike left crying talking about she was scared for him. I told her not to worry about him, because he was always careful. I warned her that when they're on a mission, his phone will be off for a while, but he always turns it back on when he's finished with the task.

"I want you and Damien to stay over here until he comes back so you're around us." I told her, listening to her cry.

The next day, all of us went out to lunch, when Candace noticed a car parked outside the restaurant. It could've been any car, but call it her intuition, she knew something was off. She called Darrell and told him what was going on, and he told her that he was on his way. Darrell was taking forever, and we noticed the car was gone, so we walked out. Jess drove Mike's truck with Alicia, and Candace and I rode together. It happened so fast that there was no way anyone could've saw it coming.

Jessica

I can't believe that Mike was going to be gone for a week. I was so used to being with him 24/7, and I didn't even know how I was going to sleep without him lying next to me. It was 11:30, and Mike called me and told me they made it to their destination safely. We talked for a little while before he said he was going to sleep, because he had to get up early to handle shit, so he could get back to me.

"I'm glad you and Damien stayed at Jas's house. That will let me know you are having some fun."

"Yea, she offered, and if I would've said no, she either would've yelled at me, or called you. I don't know why they took me under their wing, but I feel like I've known them for a long time and that they're my big sisters."

"I know they love you like a sister now, so you can't leave me if you wanted to. They won't allow you. How do you think I won you back? Those are my sisters, and they will always have your back or else."

"Ok, baby, Jas is calling me downstairs, because she and Damien rented some movie, and she screaming that I'm missing it. Shit, they even got Ms. D down there watching it with us. Baby, please be safe. I love you." I blew kisses in the phone.

"Goodnight, baby. I love you. Sunday is right around the corner, and I'm going to be there before you wake up. I promise."

I went downstairs and saw Damien lying in Jasmine's arms, watching Shrek 2. He started dozing off, but Jas wouldn't let me take him upstairs. Talking about he can go up when we do. The three of us stayed up all night talking about the guys, life, Mike's mom, and other shit. I stayed at Jasmine's house for the week. The night before Mike was supposed to come back, we went to bed after two.

Mike called me Saturday morning to tell me that he was on his way out and that his phone would be off, but he would call me as soon as he was done. Candace knocked on the door around, and rushed me to get dressed, because her and Alicia's high ass was starving.

Ms. D came and took Damien downstairs earlier to feed him. I had to say that Mike was right when he said his family would be there to help. All the kids were running wild, when I walked downstairs to give Damien a kiss before leaving. I told the girls to hold on, so I ran back upstairs to do something.

I locked the bathroom door, pulled my pants down, opened my legs, and took some pictures to send to my man. I took my shirt off and sent him pictures of my stomach that had just formed a little. You couldn't tell as much as Jas, but we were excited to be having twins. We didn't tell anyone yet; we wanted to be sure, because the doctor said that he heard two heartbeats. He wanted to do another ultrasound. He only saw one baby, but the other one was probably hiding.

I fixed myself up and went to lunch with the girls smiling. I knew my man would always be thinking about me no matter where he went. When that phone cuts back on, he will see what he left behind. I drove Mike's truck with Alicia, and the other two rode together. We got to Applebee's around 12:30, and sat there bullshitting around when Candace noticed a car sitting outside. I don't know why she was fixated on the car, but she called Darrell, and he was supposed to be on his way.

A half hour past, when Candace noticed that the car was gone and that Darrell was taking forever, so we decided to leave. Candace already told us about the tongue-lashing she was going to dish out to him. We had to park on the street, because it was the lunch hour, and there was no parking. I unlocked the car doors and reached for my phone that was ringing in my purse. Jas and Candace were in the car waiting on us, when I stepped off the curb. I looked at the phone and saw it was my mom calling.

I went to open the door, and that was the last thing I remembered before everything went black. I woke up in the hospital with no memory of what had happened and with no one around me. I was scared, nervous, and looking for my family. I could hear voices, but I couldn't speak. I thought I heard my mom arguing with someone, but my mom was like me, she didn't get into shit with nobody, so it must've been someone else. My heart started racing as I heard Mike and Damien screaming Ma-Ma. I couldn't do anything or say anything, and thought that I was dreaming, so it was only right to go to sleep.

Mike

Jess and I just found out we were having twins, and I must say that that was going to be something trying to raise three kids. I hadn't told Jess yet, but we were going house shopping when we got back. That going from house to house was a mess, and she could move her mom in as well. I knew that she was a momma's girl, and I wouldn't dare try to interrupt that. We were so used to sleeping together that it was going to be hard trying to sleep without her for a few days.

We got to Virginia earlier than expected and went out to find a seafood place to eat at. We smoked the whole way and had the munchies like a motherfucker. I told Alicia that she needed to stop, but we were just as bad. We woke up lighting up and went to sleep doing the same shit. I knew that Jess wasn't going to have that shit when we moved in together. I was going to have a shed built in the back with a man cave in it. Shit, with three kids, I knew that Jess and I were going to both need that.

The person we were meeting with called to say that she got off early, and she met us at Red Lobster. That was the closest thing to seafood we got being as though we weren't from there and had no clue where the good spots were. When she walked in, Mo and I had to take a double look, because that woman was the spitting image of Jas, as if they were twins themselves. Mo and I stood up extending our hands for introductions and sat down.

That woman was beautiful with her denim jeans, a black sweater that hung off her shoulder, some riding boots, long black hair, and a black Prada bag. She introduced herself and told us in detail what happened to her and the people that were responsible for not putting that man in jail. She gave us all the information we needed before saying that she wanted to be there to do it herself. She did a stakeout of the house for the last two weeks, when she knew we were coming.

"I'm down if you are, Mike. I mean, shit, it will be like the bad boys movie with the three of us."

"That's fine, but you will need to be ready when you get the call from one of us. We need to stakeout the place for the next few days. I know you said he has the same daily schedule, but I want to be sure since this is last minute. I want to be sliding back up in my girl by Sunday morning." I spoke firmly to her, so that she knew we meant business.

I wasn't down to do work with anyone but my brothers, but if she fucked up, she was as good as dead, so I wasn't not worried. We sat and chatted a little while longer with her before taking the information she gave us and started to do what was needed.

We put the first address in the GPS and headed over there. We did our surveillance until about one in the morning and called it a night. The next day, we went back to the house that morning, and the maid let us in once we paid her five hundred dollars. We told her that we were from the cable company. RiRi was able to get a friend to lend us a company van from Direct TV.

She noticed us looking around instead of going to the TV in the living room.

"What the fuck y'all really want?"

"Look lady, ain't nobody going to hurt you. All you have to do is leave the door unlocked Saturday for us." Mo walked into the kitchen, where her purse was, took out her license, and read off the address.

"Boy, give me back my shit. I don't care if you kill my boss. I've watched him take bribes, cheat, lie, and get people out of jail that don't deserve it. I want another thousand dollars; I'll be sure to leave the house unlocked." She said, in her Spanish accent. We couldn't believe her ass was down with it.

"You only want a thousand dollars for this."

"Yea, I don't want much. They both are unfaithful, and pay me well on the side to keep my mouth shut. I'm going to put that in my grandson's account. He is in in college and always asking me for money, so why not?"

"Shit, this was easier than we thought it would be." We ended up giving her five stacks and thanked her. She smiled and gave us the code to the house.

We walked all through the house noticing he had no video cameras, no weapons, or anything. Who was that corrupt, but didn't protect his own family? He was a dumb motherfucker.

After all the checking was done, we left and made plans to do it Saturday.

We didn't rent a hotel room, because my mom had a timeshare there, and we just used it under a different name. If anything ever came back, people from all over went there during the year, and they wouldn't know where to look first. I talked to Jess for a few and went to bed for the few hours that we were even going to get.

The day after, I called and reminded her my phone would be off, but I promised to call her as soon as I shut it back on. When we walked outside, RiRi was waiting, dressed in all black, smoking a cigarette.

"Let's do this." She said, walking to the U-Haul rental we had. We all went out to breakfast to buy some time, waiting on his wife to leave at one. Every Saturday, his wife and kid would go play tennis, and the nanny would watch the kid, which meant no one was there but him. The maid came, picked up the kid, and left.

We pulled the truck up, looked around, and walked inside. The dude was sitting in the living room watching TV, when she hit him over the head with the gun that we knew nothing about. Mo and I dragged him to the kitchen and tied his ass to a chair. I didn't want to be there long, so I threw some water on him waiting for him to open his eyes. He looked in her eyes and knew exactly who she was and why she was there.

"I'm sorry, he threatened my family. Please, I'll give you money." He said, crying and watching her put the silencer on the gun. She made sure that it was tight and put it to his head.

"Now, tell me why the fuck you represented a rapist? You made him seem like the victim. You called me all kinds of whores and said I asked for it. Now, I'm going to ask you one more time why did you represent him?" I could see Mo looking around the house, as his ass walked in the kitchen to get something to drink.

"Ok, we have to hurry up, before the wife comes back with the kid. Now, do it so we can get the fuck out of here." I told her nervous ass. She shot him right between the eyes and emptied the entire clip in his body. Let's go to the next house, and then y'all can be out." She said, wiping her eyes and walking out.

Mo and I wiped everything down and drove to the next victim's house. She was out in the yard by herself, and she lived on a dead end street. This crazy bitch jumped out the car and handled this one better. I think the initial kill had her stuck, but after she did it, she couldn't wait to come back with us to Jersey for her last one. After she ended the judge's life, we jumped in the truck, and went back to the house. She followed us to drop the U-Haul off, then we picked her FBI lieutenant husband up and headed to Jersey.

We had her drive, because we needed some sleep. We chatted it up, smoked a little weed, and dozed off. Mo was shaking the shit out of me trying to wake me up.

"Yo', where we at? We in Jersey, yet?" I asked, looking around, trying to see where we were.

"No nigga, we at the Maryland house. You hungry?"

"Oh shit, I forgot to turn my phone on. Jess is going to kill me. Yo', your phone on." I said to Mo, who was now looking at the board at the McDonald's inside.

"Nah, my phone dead. I thought you had yours on. Now, I'm going to hear that shit, too." When my phone turned on, I was ordering my food, when I noticed that it wouldn't stop vibrating. I paid for my food and noticed that I had 45 text messages, 30 voicemails, and 4 picture messages.

"Yo, what the fuck man? Look at all these messages. Something ain't right." I told Mo, walking back to the car. When I checked the first message, it was Jess saying that she loved me, and she was sending me pussy shots making me smile. After that, I got messages from my sisters telling me something had happened to Jess, and asking where the hell I was; I needed to get to the hospital and there were voicemails saying the same thing. The last text message hit me the hardest.

"How's that for always being two steps ahead of me."

"Yo', give me the keys. We have to go. Mo, take my phone, and call Jas."

I took off down 195 speeding to get back to Jersey. Mo called Jas and put her on speakerphone, when I was hit with a ton of bricks, as she tried to describe to me what happened through the cries. I almost lost control of the car when she said she hadn't woken up yet. I saw the chic in the backseat cover her mouth in shock.

"It was Ty. I know it was. The last thing I said to him was we are always two steps ahead of you, and he sent me a text that said how's that for always being two steps ahead of me? How can this one nigga cause so much pain? I can tell you why; we should've killed him the first day he came to pick Jas up. That would've avoided all of this shit." I said, still speeding and watching out for cops. It took us another hour-and-a-half to get there, but I couldn't believe how she looked.

She had a neck brace on, tubes in her nose and throat, an IV in her arm, heart monitors, blood pressure machines, a brace on both of her legs, a cast on her arm, bandages wrapped around her head, and scratches on her face. She looked so bad that I knew she had lost the babies. All I could do was stand there and cry, as her mom came and hugged me. I heard my ignorant ass mom coming down the hall talking about where is her son.

"Oh, my God, I'm glad you weren't there. I knew she was no good for you. It was probably somebody she cheated on you with." She said, pissing me off even more. I couldn't even deal with her right now, so I grabbed Damien from Candace and walked away.

"Hi, who are you? I'm Jessica's mom." She said, fixing her glasses and standing up.

"Oh, so you're her mother. Well, I'm happy my son wasn't with her. I told her not to have my son caught up in no shit with her, or we would have a problem."

Jess's mom stood up and stood face-to-face with my mom.

"Let me tell you something, Ms. Watson. That is your name, right? Don't you ever come in here talking shit about my daughter, again? She is in love with your son, and she doesn't sleep around, so stop insinuating that this is her fault." She said, before my mom tried to cut her off. "No, I'm still speaking. My daughter told me how you treated her, and I said that, maybe she took it the wrong way, but seeing it for myself, I see that you are a bitter and ignorant woman.

You so far up that other chic, Maria's, ass, trying to get her back with Mike, that you are trying to destroy what they have. Yea, I know, because Maria's mom goes to church with me, and she raves about how you got her living with you now that she came back and how you are working on getting them back together.

Your son loves my daughter, and the faster you realize that, the better, but I tell you one damn thing, God don't like ugly, and if you say one more thing about my daughter, I'm whooping your ass. Don't let me going to church fool you. Now, get the fuck out of here. Security, please escort her ass out of here, and if I hear she came by my daughter's room, because she works here, I will sue this fucking hospital. Lord, forgive me for cursing. I'm sorry Mike and Mo, but the devil took over me." She said, walking back over to Jasmine, holding her hand.

I couldn't do nothing but shake my head. That was what my mom got, and I couldn't have said that shit any better.

"Ma, tell me that shit ain't true about Maria living there, and you trying to get us back together."

"Boy, grow up. That woman Maria loves you, and now that Jessica most likely lost the babies, that is the only baby mom you have." She said, rolling her eyes. I almost lost it on her ass. Cornell and Darrell had to hold me back, so that Mo could walk her out.

I picked Damien up and walked over to Jess when he screamed out MaMa. I sat down in the chair next to her mom, as everyone else tried to fit into the room. The girls stayed with me all night, as her mom took Damien home, because it was getting late.

"I'm sorry that I had to disrespect your mom like that Mike. You know that's not me, but as a mother, I could not allow her to go on about Jess." I put him in the car seat, walked around the car, and kissed her cheek.

"She deserved it. I will never get mad at you for defending your daughter. I just wish Jess would do the same sometimes for herself. I love you, and I'll call if anything changes before morning."

I walked back in and noticed that the girl and her husband were still there. I told them to leave and said to come back tomorrow to meet the squad.

Jas and Alicia were laid out on the bed with Jess the best they could, and Candace laid the chair out for herself.

"Where the fuck y'all think I'm sleeping at?" I said, as the nurse came and said that they were moving her upstairs. We got to her room, and there was no patient in the other bed, so I sent their asses over there, and I got into the bed with my baby. This was going to be a long journey.

Candace

I couldn't sleep at all, and I saw Mike watching TV, so I tapped him on the leg and told him let's go smoke. He told the nurses that we were going downstairs but that her sisters were in the room with her if they needed anything. He also told them no one is to go in that room without him knowing about it first. We got downstairs and took a walk up the street, because we knew the weed would smell. Mike was so deep in thought that, when I looked at him, he was crying. I couldn't imagine the pain that he was going through right now, and I didn't want to try. I passed him the blunt, wiping the tears from his eyes.

"Sis, I need you to tell me word for word what happened, and don't leave shit out, even if you think I don't want to hear it.

I told him that Jess stepped off the curb to walk to the car when we all heard a screech, causing us to look back. It was too late, as the person came flying down the street, side swiping the car, with Jess trying to get in the truck, but it was too late. Her body was hit and flew in the air, landing on the top of the truck before sliding off. We all jumped out of the car, rushing to Jess, when whoever that was stopped until I started walking to the car with my gun in hand.

"Mike, it doesn't seem like this was a random accident at all. After we saw that car, I knew that something was up, but when the car disappeared, we thought it was ok to leave. I didn't know who would've done something like this. Especially, to her." I told him, with tears coming down my face.

"What happened to Darrell? Why didn't he make it in time? Where was he?" He asked me, wiping his eyes with the back of his hands.

"He got into a fender bender rushing to get there. He said the person was being over dramatic, so he had to wait for the cops and ambulance to arrive and file a report. He was so mad because the person hit him, and he knew something wasn't right when I called. You know Darrell is laid back and won't say much, but he wouldn't stop cursing when he arrived on the scene. The cops almost arrested his ass for trying to pick Jess up himself and take her to the hospital, saying the EMT's were taking too long." I told him.

"That's my nigga. I would've done the same."

Mike, after she was hit, she called out for you and Damien. All she kept saying was, please tell my mom to take care of my son, and don't tell Mike. He is going to be so mad that his truck got fucked up. When she said, "Why are y'all crying, I'm going to be fine," it was as if she couldn't feel the pain that we knew she was in. We kept talking to her when her eyes started fluttering, rolling in the back of her head.

98

They had to take Jas in another ambulance, because she was so hysterical that they thought she was going to pass out." I laid my head on his shoulder. We sat there a little while longer, when Alicia walked up behind us, cursing because we didn't wake her to come out.

"Hey, I guess y'all couldn't sleep, either, huh?" She said, taking a seat on the other side of Mike.

"Well, I guess her mom called Damien's dad, because he came rushing to the hospital with guess who? Yup, that bitch, Laura, that tried to kick it to you at the bar. Her face was still fucked up from whatever Jas did to her. He came in barking all these orders for tests that he wanted her to have, and those motherfuckers were doing whatever he said.

He tried to take Damien, but her mom wasn't having that shit. She was like, no, because Jess will want to see him when she gets up. I know you've only been with her a short time, but she is like our sister already, and we are going to find out who did this. I don't even think that girl has one damn enemy. Well, except for Lil' Darrell, because she wouldn't let Damien stay over the other day."

"Mike, she is going to be ok. The love she has for you and her son will not allow her to leave this earth yet." Alicia told him, laying on the other side of his shoulder.

"Hey, I need one of y'all to tell me what happened to my babies? No one seems to want to talk about it."

"First off, nigga, I want to know why you didn't tell nobody she was having twins, and second, she lost them. The

99

trauma to her body was so bad that they believe the babies died on impact. Mike, I'm so sorry. I know you wanted to be a dad, but everything happens for a reason, and it wasn't time for y'all to have babies yet. Don't worry. We know that, when she gets better, y'all going to be fucking like rabbits again, probably, getting her pregnant, immediately." Alicia said, standing up, giving him a hug.

"Yea, she's right Mike. Don't worry; we will keep Damien for a week if that's how long y'all need to be locked up in the house fucking to get pregnant again." He wiped his eyes and started walking towards the hospital.

"Yo', Jess is going to be so mad that she missed him say his first words, and it was him calling for her." I knew that Mike loved the shit out of Jess, but I didn't know how he would handle it if she died.

We walked into the room, and Jas was standing next to Jess's bed crying and smiling at the same time. Mike went rushing over to see Jess lying there with her eyes opened, pointing to the tubes in her throat. He bent down to kiss her forehead and rubbed her hair back. Jess wanted the tubes out so Alicia ran to the nurses' station, raising hell about how she pressed the button, and they should've been in there already.

Jess made a sign with her hand like she wanted to write something down. Mike took a piece of paper out of the drawer and handed her a pen. She started to write slow and a little sloppy, as we all tried to understand what she wrote.

The first note read, "Mike, was weed more important than her?" He shook his head no and asked why she asked him that. She started trying to write with force until her hand must've started to hurt, but when we read it, we looked away laughing.

It read, "Why wasn't your ass in here when I woke up then?" We couldn't do anything but laugh, because no matter how hurt she was, she still went in on him.

"Baby, I'm sorry. Candace and I couldn't sleep so we went outside to smoke." She looked over at me, and I just shrugged my shoulders and pointed to Alicia like, "she came, too". When the nurse took the tubes out of her throat, we had to look the other way. There were all kinds of shit coming out with it making Jess choke at the same time. Mike poured her some water, put the straw to her lips, and watched her drink.

"Jess, I'm so sorry I wasn't here when this happened. I wish it were me laying here instead of you, so that I could take all of your pain away. I won't ever leave you again, I promise."

We called and text everyone that she was awake. Her mom was so happy that she was up to the hospital within an hour with Damien. Mike laid him in the bed with her, but only let him stay for a few minutes, because he was getting antsy, moving all around and instilling pain. Not on purpose, of course.

Damien's dad walked in and greeted everyone, including Mike. You could tell that he still had love for Jess, but she only had eyes for Mike. He wanted to speak to everyone outside, but she didn't want Mike to walk out of the room. He kissed her and said that he was only outside the door. He told us that she was both lucky and unlucky when it came to the accident.

"I just wanted to say I'm sorry for the loss of your babies." He said to Mike, who nodded his head, not really wanting to hear that part.

He went on telling us about the injuries, but that she was lucky. He ran every test possible on her, and she would be in pain for weeks to come. She would need constant care, including baths and meals. I would take Damien for the first few days, when she got out, so that she could get comfortable at home.

"Mike, I will give you my cell, so that, if anything happens, you can call me. I hope the cops find out who did this to her." He said, before asking to speak to Mike alone. We walked back inside and kept the door cracked so that we could listen.

"Mike, I'm really sorry for your loss. She told me about the pregnancy, and she was so happy that she found someone to make her feel the way you do. Do you know she thanked me for fucking up, because God placed you in her life? I messed up bad with an amazing woman, and now, you and her have a lifetime to be amazing together.

Please take care of her. She will need you and whoever else to help her through this. She doesn't know about the babies, yet. I can tell her or you can; it's up to you." He said, extending his hand out to Mike, who in return gave him a man hug. He thanked him for everything and said that he wanted to tell her. He took down the doctor's number and told him that he would have Damien's stuff together when she was released.

"Oh yea, my man. Damien said his first words, but they were MaMa. Sorry, but that's who he chose to say first." Mike told him, as they both laughed, and he went back to work. I couldn't do anything but respect how much Mike had grown into a man thanks to Jess. If this were before, he would've told that nigga to get out of his face.

Mike lifted the bed up with the remote, so that she could see better. They had removed the neck brace late last night when the results came back that it wasn't broke, but she still couldn't turn it as fast.

It was ten o' clock when the hospital room was filled with all my kids, Alicia's daughter, Damien, all the guys, and us. Jessica looked around the room and started crying. Mike asked why she was crying and when she wrote because all these people are here for me.

"Girl, didn't I tell you, you are now our family, too? Even if you leave Mike's ass, again, we still going to be your sisters. Don't you ever forget that."

Malika chimed in. "Yes, Aunty Jess. Who else is going to teach me Spanish? Aunty Licia can't speak it as well as you. She can only understand it."

"Mommy, is Aunty Jess going to be alright." One of my kids asked. See girl, these kids already know you as Aunty Jess, and they love you and Damien just like we do. And, we wouldn't have it any other way, so stop crying. You trying to make the whole room tear up."

When Maria, his mom, and Devon walked in the door, the whole room got quiet, and I knew right then this was going to be a problem.

Mo

I like Jess for Mike, because she makes him a better person, and if anyone can do that for him, that was whose team I was on. Even though we were twins, he has always been the hotheaded one that didn't ask questions at all; he just did the shooting. But that was my brother, and no matter what, I would always have his back.

When we were standing in the line at the rest stop, and he wanted to know if my phone was on, I could tell he was a little nervous. It was like he knew something wasn't right. My brother had an instinct that, when it was a bad one, we wouldn't act on whatever we were about to do. His instinct kept us out of a lot of shit when we were on our missions, causing us to stay longer than anticipated to finish a job.

I could see the fear in his eyes when he turned his phone on and saw all the messages and voicemails that he had missed. He handed me his phone for me to call Jas, as he took off down I95, and I didn't blame him. I would've done the same thing had that been Jas. When Jas started trying to tell us what happened, I couldn't believe that that nigga went that far. Now, it was war. I knew that Mike was mad, because he was talking about how we should've never let him date Jas from the start. Mike was on a mission from here on out, and I didn't feel one ounce of sorry for Ty, because he had this day coming.

We got to the hospital and asked registration where Jess was at in the back. Thank goodness they put her in one of the rooms, because it was so many of us there. The female and her husband that rode with us stayed in the waiting room. The site of Jess was ten times worse than the sight that I saw Jas in when she was violated. I don't even know how she was breathing on her own by the way the way she was hooked up to everything. I'd never seen my brother cry, so to see him break down had my heart aching for him. I pulled Jas close to me and hugged her so tight, thanking the Lord that it wasn't her. I know that there was no way Jess didn't lose the baby. I saw my mom walking down the hall out the corner of my eye, and I knew she was about to make a scene.

She started going in on how this was Jess's fault, and thank goodness Mike wasn't there. He couldn't take that shit, picked up my nephew Damien, and walked down the hall, but when Jess's mom stood up and told my mother off, I couldn't do anything but turn my head and laugh. Jas looked up at me and smacked my arm, but deep down, she knew my mother deserved that shit.

Unfortunately, I think my mom lost a son in that hospital that night. Once Mike found out that she secretly had Maria living there and was trying to get them back together, he was so mad. What threw him over was when she basically said that Jess wasn't pregnant no more, so he should be with Maria.

Cornell and Darrell had to hold that nigga back from jumping on my mom, and I just stood there and watched. Everything she said had consequences, and she would deal with not having a son.

I walked her out to the car and saw the tears running from her eyes, but I didn't feel bad for her at all. She deserved everything that happened and that was said to her. When she got to the car, she turned around and gave me a big hug apologizing to me for the way she treated Jas. She started trying to do the same for Mike, but I told her that she had to talk to him about that.

"Son, I'm sorry if I treated your woman like shit. I don't mean to. I just want y'all to be happy, and I want you with the right woman. I may come off wrong to them, but it's just to let them know that I don't play with my sons. I can't believe Mike was going to attack me over that girl. I guess he really does love her. Huh?" She asked me, wiping her eyes.

"Yea, Ma. He is head over heels in love with her. He just wanted you to get to know her before you started judging, but you snapped on her the very first day. You didn't even give her a chance to piss you off. Then, you acting as if you cared that she was pregnant but disrespected her son. Mike is hurting right now, and all he needs is his mom, but you took him to a place that I never thought I would see. My brother is hurting, Ma, and I'm going back in to be by his side. I'll see you tomorrow."

"Yo', this nigga has to go." Mike stated, as I nodded my head. He walked back in, because no other words needed to be spoken. I went to the back to get Jas.

"Baby, I think I'm going to stay the night with the girls. Are you ok with that?" She asked, standing in front of me, looking innocent.

"Come on, baby. I was going to take you off punishment today and give you the D."

"I know, baby, but I'll be home tomorrow, and we can make up for lost time then. I love you."

"I guess, but you know Mike may kick y'all asses out if you get on his nerves. I love you so much girl, and I don't know what I would do if that was you." I stood in the living room, looking around and wondering why the fuck I was still there, when I heard a knock at the door. I opened the door, and Lola was standing there, staring at me, with the most pitiful look ever.

"What up, yo? Long time, no see." I said, letting her walk right in. I know Jas would kick my ass right now if she knew this woman was here. She sat on the couch and started asking me all these questions about Jas.

"Baby, I miss you. And now I see you parading this mixed bitch all around town like you don't miss me." She whined, standing up and walking towards me. I backed up and hit the damn wall, when she opened her jacket to show me that she was completely naked underneath.

My man stood right up, and I started having flashbacks about how good she used to suck my dick. She pulled my shorts and boxers down, putting my man in her mouth. I was so horny from putting Jas on punishment, and then, she stayed at the hospital; this was so-needed.

"Yea, I know just how daddy likes it. Mmmm, yea, cum for me." She said, in between sucking and slurping. It was feeling so good that I couldn't stop her.

"Aaaaah shit, girl. Damn. You know you can suck some dick girl." I told her after she finished swallowing all my babies. She turned the stereo on, led me to the couch, and sat with her legs spread wide opened. She started jerking my dick, making him wake up, and slid the head up and down her pussy lips. I ran to my room to get a condom and started pounding that pussy in and out, making her scream my name. We fucked all over the house, and even took a shower together, just like old times. Her pussy is nowhere near as good as Jas', but I needed some ass, and Jas should've came home.

We fell asleep afterwards, but I woke her ass up around six and told her she had to go. I took another shower to wash Lola off me, and when I let that water hit, my body regretted every bit of what I did.

It was too late for regrets now. I knew I should've never allowed her in, but thinking with my dick had gotten me in some shit. I went to see Darrell, because I knew that he would understand with all the shit him and Candace went through. I pulled up at the garage and saw some of my boys outside. I kicked it with them for a few before I went in to talk to Darrell.

"Yo', what up. I am on my way to the hospital. You want to ride over with me?" He asked, as I hopped in the car doing my normal.

"Man, I fucked up last night." I told him, puffing and looking out the window.

"What's up? What did you do now?"

"Lola came over last night talking about how she missed me and some other shit. The crazy thing is, when she opened her coat, she was butt ass naked, and I was ok with that, but she started licking her lips and dropped to her knees, and that was all she wrote. After that, we fucked all through the house and even in the shower.

We fell asleep, but I threw her ass out around six, just in case Jas decided to come. It was crazy. It was like I didn't think about hurting Jas one bit until I woke up this morning. Does that mean I don't love Jas?"

"Yo', I can't believe you man. This shit is going to cause havoc at my house when she finds out, and you know she will, because Lola has always wanted to be your woman. I'm telling you to tell Jas before she finds out, so that you can deal with the consequences and move on. Jas will not take it well coming from someone else. Man, that's all the advice I can give you. I love you, though, man. I'll be praying for you. Shit, you saw how they came together when they thought Mike cheated on Jess; I can't imagine what they're going to do to you.

Jessica

I woke up again trying to figure out what happened to me, when Jas came off the other bed to check on me. She started crying when she saw that my eyes were open and started pressing the button for the nurses. I think that I was closest to Jas than I was the other two; probably because we were dating twins and pregnant together. I needed this damn nurse to come in and take this shit out of my throat.

I wanted to ask Mike why he wasn't there when I woke up, but couldn't speak, so he gave me paper to write it. He threw Candace under the bus with him, and she threw Alicia in it. I wanted to see my son, but was unsure of the time. I pointed to my wrist to ask for the time, and it was 6:30 in the morning, so I had Mike call my mom to bring Damien up, and the girls called everybody else.

They spoke about my condition for when I left, I told him I'm glad he fucked up. I got a kick out of that, because I was sure that Mike loved hearing that shit, but it was true. At ten o' clock, everyone was in my hospital room, when Mike's mom walked in with that bitch, Maria, and I'm assuming, her son. The heart monitor started beeping faster, as Mike looked up and saw why.

"I'm going to ask you nicely to leave, and I don't want to cause a scene in front of Devon, but I will."

"I just wanted to say that I'm so sorry this happened to you. I know we didn't start off on the right foot, but I really thought that Mike and I could work it out. I kept getting these messages on Facebook from one of his friends saying he wanted to be with me, and that was really why I came back.

After that stuff happened at his house, I went to his mom's and told her. She offered me to stay there, because my mom only lived in a one bedroom, and there was no room. I'm not going to lie, I still love him, and always will, but after seeing you two at the club, I knew you had his heart. The love I saw in both of your eyes showed me that there was nothing that I could do to break that. I didn't deserve to be spit on, but the ass whooping, I knew was coming. Those are his sisters, and they've always had his back, so I didn't expect anything differently." She said, looking at Candace and Alicia, who nodded their heads.

"I see now that they have taken you under their wing, and I can respect that. All I ask is that, now that we're back, don't keep Mike from his son. I did some shit in the past to him that I now regret, but I have to live with the choices I made. But if this is who he's going to be with, I would rather be cordial and not an enemy." Devon walked to sit on Mike's mom's lap, who was now sitting down in front of me. I asked Mike for some paper to write something.

"I appreciate you coming here, and I will never keep them apart. We can finish this conversation another day, because this takes too long." Mike read it out loud, as everyone started laughing.

"Let's go back to saying someone hit you up on Facebook saying I wanted you to come back. Do you know who it was? What was his screen name?" Mike asked her, and I was listening too. She tried to pull the person up, but she couldn't find him. She did screenshot the messages, because she knew Mike wouldn't believe her. When he looked at the messages, he saw that dude knew all his business an even sent her a plane ticket. He was furious, because he knew her coming to the house was a set-up to destroy our relationship.

"Mike and Jess, I want to say I'm sorry." His mom stood up and said, making everybody stop talking and look up. I thought Mike wanted her back, because she told me all that she told you. I know I should've listened to you, because you are my son. Jessica, the way I treated you was unacceptable, and I hope you can forgive me, but if you can't, I understand.

After your mom went off on me, I knew I was dead wrong, and I would've reacted the same way had that been my daughter. I just want what's best for my sons, and if you are what he wants, then I will respect that. I never had my son raise his voice or even his hand to me over a woman. He was ready to lose me for you, and that showed me that you are the woman that he loves."

She walked over, gave me a hug, and then, gave Mike one. I could tell that he didn't really want to hug her, but I gave him a look. Since he didn't want to upset me, he just did it, but him and his mom had to talk about that shit.

They left not too long after, then my mom and Ms. D took the kids home, because they were running everywhere. They needed some space to run, and this was not the place. I wrote to Mike that I wanted to be washed, so he kicked everybody out so that the nurse could give me a sponge bath and teach Mike what to do when we got home. Everyone came back in and something happened that I never thought would with Mo and Jasmine.

I was so disappointed in Mo and hurt for Jas that I cried as the video when the pictures were sent to my phone. Mike stood over my bed, looking in my phone, and snatched it out my hand. He looked at Mo and shook his head in disgust. Jasmine flipped, and the girls jumped Mo right in my hospital room. I couldn't believe so much had happened in one day to destroy a family.

Ty

After I left the hospital from being shot by that dumb ass nigga, I was stuck in there for two days. I found out where Mike's girl lived, because I had plans for her, and I knew this plan would fuck him up royally. I watched his girl go to lunch with my baby Jasmine and the other tricks. I watched them go in and that nosy bitch Candace must've noticed my car, as I watched her keep looking out the window.

I moved down the street a little and sat there waiting for them to come out. I was hoping that Jas would get in the car so that I can do what I needed to do. Jess was looking down, as I eased up the road slowly, but sped up when I saw her step off that curb. She didn't even see me coming, as I rode close to the car hitting Jess and watching her body fly in the air like a bird soaring. She hit the top of the truck so hard that I knew she had to be dead.

I felt bad watching my baby hyperventilate after seeing her new friend hit the truck like that. I wanted to get out and comfort her, but I couldn't when I saw that bitch sister of hers walking to my car with a gun. I peeled out of there fast as hell, not wanting to die, because I needed to finish causing damage.

I went to the closest bar to get a quick drink to celebrate that I knew I had one brother down and one to go. The funny thing was running into Lola, who was there with a few of her friends. I sent a drink her way, and when she looked up, I nodded my head and smiled. I knew that she would come over soon enough to thank me. A few minutes later, she walked over to speak.

"Thank you for the drink. I appreciate it. My name is Lola, and you are?" She asked me, extending her hand. We ended up talking about life, and then, she remembered me from the BBQ.

"Oh, you're the guy that was with that bitch Jas, who stole my man, Mo." She sipped her drink. "I'm going to get my man back. Fuck that bitch. I know what he wants and needs. She could never do for him what I can."

"Well lady. Jasmine is my girl, and I believe we could help one another out. Are you down for that?" I quizzed her to see if she would be down. After we talked a little while longer, we came up with a plan. As a man, we knew that he would fall for it.

That same day, we exchanged phone numbers to get Mo's ass. It was 10:30 when Mo pulled up to his condo, as Lola and I watched him unlock the door and close it. I sent Lola in and told her to make sure the door was unlocked. Five minutes had passed, when I noticed the lights dim. I walked to the condo, looking around and making sure no one saw me and would call the cops.

I waited a little while longer before I walked in. I had to admit that Mo had his condo laid out, as I looked around for a few seconds and remembered what I was there for. I heard them in the back room, so I walked back there, and the door was cracked open, and Lola was riding Mo's dick, while he had his eyes closed. I snapped a few pictures of him in that position, hitting Lola from the back, and I even got a few of them in the shower. I snapped a few more pictures around the house, so Jas saw that it was not a hotel he was at, but at one of the homes they shared. I knew this was going to hurt Jas, but she needed to know the kind of man she had.

I left Lola's ass there, because all the fucking they were doing, I damn sure, wasn't sitting out there all night. It was noon the next day, and I knew all those motherfuckers were at the hospital. It was time to set fire under his ass. I bought a prepaid cell and sent all the pictures to that phone, and then, hit send to Jas and everyone else.

"Is this the man you plan on spending the rest of your life with?"

I sent a text to Lola and told her to start her part of the plan, which was to post a few pictures of Mo sleeping next to her. She posted a bunch of different pictures on Instagram.

"Yea, bitch, that's my man lying next to me. I put that ass to sleep."

I monitored the IG, watching all the likes that she was getting, when I noticed a comment from Jas. I was shocked that they were even friends on there, but I figured that they met at the BBQ, and probably, just didn't delete one another.

It read, "Baby, you can have him, but what you should've done was come to me like a woman instead of letting everybody know how much of a whore you are. I will drop all his shit off to your house; I hope y'all live a long life together."

Jasmine

When the guys got back to the hospital, they brought my sisters and me clothes, and we all took showers in Jess' bathroom. The nurse threw all of us out around 11:30, so that she could give Jess a sponge bath and show Mike and her mom how to do it for when she left. Mike refused to have her sitting in the hospital without washing and looking a fucking mess. Ms. D took Ms. Gomez with her back to the house with all the kids, because they were becoming restless.

We all walked back in when they were done, and I sat on Mo's lap, and thought I noticed a hickey on his neck. I knew that that wasn't possible, because we hadn't fucked, and I knew he hadn't cheat on me. Jess was more alert and starting to get her voice back, but still was writing, and Mike was so happy.

My phone started going off non-stop, and when I looked down to reach for it, Mo was looking at his phone, too. Mo looked like he saw a ghost and told me not to check my phone; trying to take it out my hand.

"Yo', why is that bitch Lola tagging me in her shit on Instagram? We ain't even cool like that." Candace said, as Alicia and I walked over to see what was tagged on the page.

My hands started shaking, as I covered my mouth, looking at the pictures of Mo laid up in the bed naked.

"Jas, let me talk to you." I started crying, hysterically, and throwing anything I could at him. "Calm the fuck down now Jas. I'm not playing with you. Let me talk to you." He gritted through his teeth.

Just then, my phone went off again, and what I saw on the phone had me crying harder. No one really knew what the hell I had on my phone until Candace picked it up, pressed play on the video, and you heard Lola screaming Mo's name.

Alicia told Candace to turn it off, as they both started jumping Mo right in front of me. Mo wouldn't hit them back, because he didn't beat on woman, but Cornell and Darrell picked them both up and held them back. Jess started crying, as she took her hand to cover her mouth, when she witnessed the video. It was as if the video and pictures were sent to everyone in that room at the exact same time.

"After everything I have been through. I mean everything; you go and do this to me? I can't even say this is old, because that's the new furniture, and those are the clothes you had on yesterday right here. See, even though she was being a bitch, she made sure to send me pictures of the entire house, letting me know that she's been there, so you couldn't say she was lying. I admit, nigga, you had me fooled. You really did. I thought I was seeing things when I looked at what appeared to be this hickey on your neck." I yelled, pointing my finger to the spot. He moved my hand, looking at me with regret in his eyes, but I wasn't trying to hear anything he had to say.

"See, I'm not going to fight for you, because you didn't fight for us. There's no way you can say you love me when you fucked her in, what seems to be, all night, because you were sleep in this picture. But the sad part is that you thought you wouldn't get caught. Oh, and you definitely enjoyed it, because as she says, "She put that ass to sleep. In saying that, the best woman has won, and she can have your trifling ass." He stood there looking stupid.

"Let this shit right here marinade in your brain, though. When you see me with another nigga I'm going to let him fuck me so good that I'm screaming out his name, and you can bet, I'll make sure you get a copy of the video." I thought he was going to strangle me when I said that by the way the guys had to hold him back.

"I hope y'all are happy together, because this right here, my nigga, IS OVER!!!!!! I hate you." I did the ultimate disrespect by hocking and spitting in his face. Then, I started walking out the door, laughing, but hurting. He tried to walk after me, but Mike got up this time and walked in front of him. I turned around, with tears falling down my face. "I'm so sorry Jess, but I can't be here right now. I will come see you when he's not here. I love you, and get better soon, so we can sit up late night again."

"If you try and come to my house Mo, I will shoot your ass where you stand. I love you, Mike, Darrell and Cornell, and I hope you understand when I say don't bring his ass to my fucking house, and don't call me for or about him. Call his new bitch. I'm out." I stated, walking out the door with Alicia and Candace right behind me. I could tell that Mo was burning a hole in my back, as I walked out, because I could still hear the guys telling Mo to just leave me alone.

I cried hysterically in the car having flashbacks of what Jess was probably going through when she thought Mike cheated. The only difference was that Mo did, and the proof was right in front of me. I couldn't get the images out of my head of him fucking her. She was screaming his name like he was giving it to her the way he used to with me.

When Alicia pulled up to the house, I told her to wait in the car, and that I needed to do something. We knew where Lola lived, because it was a small town, and everybody knew one another. I grabbed all Mo's stuff from my house, even his toothbrush, and had Alicia drive over to her house. I was going to have her come pick it up, but this needed to be done. We all got out, and Alicia rang the doorbell and waited for her to answer. I could tell that she was nervous, because she kept the chain on the door and asked what we wanted.

"Lola, since you wanted Mo so bad, you can have him. I figured I'd drop his stuff off to you since, we aren't together anymore. I hope that you feel real good about yourself breaking up somebody's home." I said, handing her his stuff, after she took the chain off and opened the door.

"Well, he didn't look at it like it was his home, because I wouldn't have been able to break it up." She sounded cocky as hell, as she said it.

"You're right. And you don't owe me shit. That's why I can't be mad at you. You're a woman who wanted something and went out and got it. I can respect that, but what I can't respect is the way you went about it. All you had to do was hit me up, and we could've discussed it like women. Instead, you tried to embarrass me by tagging all of us in it. And, because of that, my sisters have to give you the ass whooping you deserve for posting that shit and tagging us all in it.

"Oh, you have four more months to have him to yourself before his baby arrives. Yes, I'm pregnant so even though you did that, you will never be first in his life. Have a good life with him, and pray that another woman doesn't do to you what you've done to me. And for the record, he told me you guys weren't a couple before we fucked." I yelled back, walking away, watching Darrell and Mo pull up. *Damn, they must've known I was coming over here.*

"Jas, please let me talk to you." He said over and over, grabbing my arm, as I walked to the car.

"I loved you in hopes that you loved me back. There was nothing I wouldn't have done for you. I would've died for you, and you know that, because I almost did. I chose love, and you didn't, so please accept that, and leave me alone." I tried to walk away, but he kept holding me.

"Mo, listen. You took my heart, stepped on it, kicked it, and tossed it out for here, but with all my flaws and issues, you couldn't hold it down for me, and I can't be with a man that jumps at the first sight of pussy when his girl ain't around. I'm sorry Mo. This can never ever be." I pulled him close, kissed him on the lips, with tears pouring down my face like rain and jumped in the car. I watched my sisters wipe their eyes, as they felt my pain, being as though they went through it before with their men.

Moe

When Lola sent me pictures of us last night, before I could send her ass a message back, Jas' phone went off. Then Candace said that Lola tagged her in a picture. I tried to snatch Jas' phone before she could see anything, but it was too late. Candace opened the IG, and there was a picture of me and Lola laid out in the bed. The hurt I saw wash over Jas' face killed me, and there was nothing I could do to stop it. She opened up a video, and you could hear skin smacking, and Lola screaming out my name. Jas started tossing shit all around the room and slid down the wall crying. The girls started punching me all over, but it didn't matter. I let them, as I watched Jas. She got up off the floor, grabbed her stuff, hock spit in my face, and left.

I grabbed Darrell and asked him to drive me by Lola's house, because I saw Jas post under the picture for her to pick my stuff up. I knew Jas better, and she wasn't letting her come to her house. When we got there, it was too late; the girls had already beat Lola's ass. That was what her ass got for opening her damn mouth and taking pictures.

"I never thought I would lose her, man. I should've just listened to you and told her. How could I be stupid and fuck that girl? Jas had everything I needed and more. I was being selfish, so I guess I have to take this shit." I told Darrell, as we rode to the garage, so that I could pick my car up.

"Man, I hate to say I told you so, but I did. I mean, you told me a while back that Lola had mediocre pussy, so you risked all that for some mediocre shit? I know I did some shit in the past, and we got through it, but I would never put Candace through anymore shit like that again. We fought; she cheated after I did, and the cycle got so bad that she was going to leave me, but we had so many years in to make it work.

I don't know what to tell you to do. I saw how bad Jas was hurt, and I don't think she will ever forgive you, but hey, I thought Candace wouldn't, and she did. Just give it some time, and talk to your sisters. They may be able to help you get Jas back like Mike got Jess back. Let me ask you this? Do you want Jas back, or do you want to be with Lola?" He asked me, and I couldn't get mad, because I should have known better.

"I love Jas so much, and I don't know why I was thinking with my dick. I really don't. I wish I could redo the whole night and take it all back, but I can't. I want to marry Jas, but that's not going to happen. She killed me when she reminded me of how she almost died to be with me, and I chose pussy over her. That's fucked up, because she risked her life for me, and I shitted on her."

When we got to the garage, I spoke to him a little longer before leaving. My phone started ringing, and I prayed it was

Jas, but it was Candace. I just blew my breath, because most likely, she and Alicia were on their way, waiting to curse me out.

"What up, sis?"

"Not much, where are you? Alicia and I are at your house waiting for you. How long is it going to take you to get here?"

I told them ten minutes, and they said they would be there. I pulled in next to them, hopped out the car with them walking behind me in the house. I threw my keys on the kitchen counter and walked to the fridge to get a bottle of water.

"What's up? Before y'all start going in, I already know how fucked up I am, and I ain't shit." Alicia sat there, rolling the blunt while Candace took her shoes off and put her feet underneath her on the chair.

"I just want to know why? Fuck all the other shit." Candace said, throwing Alicia the lighter to spark the blunt. I went to speak, but Alicia put her finger up for me to wait, as she took a pull and passed the blunt to Candace.

"To be honest, I don't know why. She came by here last night and started talking shit about me parading Jas around, then she dropped to her knees. I should've stopped her, but I didn't, and when she sat on the couch and spread her legs, I just started fucking her." I told them, as we passed the blunt around.

"Oh shit, nigga, what couch?" They both said jumping up. I pointed to the one Alicia was sitting at. She ran into the kitchen, grabbed the Lysol, sprayed the couch, and sat next to Candace.

"So, let me get this right? You allowed my sister to almost die for you, get pregnant by you, and fall in love, before you decided to cheat on her? I mean, why not just leave? Or, why sleep with Lola at all? You had so many choices, and you chose your dick over everything. I just don't get it." Candace said to me, making me feel more like shit. We all sat looking up at the ceiling not saying a word. I just got up and went to lie down in the back. The girls came back and sat on the edge of the bed.

"I will always be team Jasmine, Mo, but what you did was unforgivable. Jas is so fragile, and you were supposed to be her protector, instead, you fed her to the wolves for some ass. I am your sister, too, but this situation is fucked up."

"I think the video made it worse by hearing Lola screaming out your name. Jas will never get that image or those pictures out of her head. I know I wouldn't be able to. To watch your man make another woman feel the same pleasures he gives you is a nightmare.

I don't think you understand the damage you did to her. Mo, you watched her fall into that deep depression when Assad died, you saved her from Ty, she gave you her heart, and this is how you repay her? I swear, I'm going to kill you if she does something to hurt herself or the baby." Candace told me, before walking out with Alicia following behind, throwing up the peace sign.

I laid there all night awake, looking at the wall. I checked Jas' IG, and instead of her deleting me, she took down all of our pictures. She put up a new photo with a caption that read, *Single again, and hating it. But we have to love ourselves before we can love someone else."*

She had over a hundred likes, and I posted, *I still love you* under her comments section and turned my phone off. There was no need to leave it on, because there was no one calling me. I fucked up bad, and I had no one to blame but myself.

Jasmine

Two months had passed since the shit happened with Mo, and he hadn't stop trying to call or text me since. Jess was released from the hospital two weeks later and told me she heard Mike cursing Mo out for doing that to me. She also told me that one of the girls that she worked with was friends with Lola and that they were still fucking. I appreciate what she told me, because every day I got stronger and figured that I could handle him if I ran into him.

The first few weeks were horrible after I saw the video. I would wake up having nightmares about that shit but each day got easier. I had to remind myself that I was pregnant, and I didn't want to lose the baby stressing over him. I posted a picture of my baby's sonogram picture on IG and tagged Mo and Lola being smart. I was starting to become excited when Ms. D offered to go to Babies' R Us with me. Mike said that he would put the crib together for me, and since I was getting the nursery together, I may as well get it.

Ms. D and I got back from Babies R Us, and I was exhausted, so I went to my room and took a nap. When I got, up the crib was already set up in the nursery, and Mike was downstairs talking to Ms. D.

"Thanks. I appreciate it. Your mom is throwing me a baby shower, and I would love it if you, Jess, Damien, and her mom came."

"Of course we'll be there. Jess' mom is making a pan of beans and rice, and Jess is making you some empanadas. Those shits are good as hell. Wait 'til you try them. I love you, sis, and you'll get through this. Call me or Jess if you need anything. I don't care what it is, day or night."

After Mike left, it was around nine, and I wanted to get some fresh air. I got in my car, drove to the beach, and sat on one of the benches. I was listening to Alicia Keys song "Try Sleeping with a Broken Heart", when someone sat next to me. I was tired of ignoring him, so I didn't move. He had on some gray sweats, a t-shirt, Air Force Ones, and a black hat, looking good enough to eat. He had me wanting to jump on him, but I didn't. I just watched him lay his head back.

"What are you doing here?"

He took one of the earplugs out and listened to the song as it played,

Even if you were a million miles away,
I still could feel you in my bed,
Near me, touch me, feel me,
And even at the bottom of the sea,

"What are you doing here, Mo?"

"I know this is your spot when you want to get away, and I figured that, since you couldn't run, you'd at least be walking. I ride by here every night hoping to run into you, and tonight, was my lucky night. I miss you so much, Jas. I don't know why I cheated, and I have no excuse for the poor choice I made. I'm not going to bother you about it, because I made my bed, and now I have to lay in it, but how are you and my baby doing?" He asked me, rubbing on my stomach and smiling. When he lifted my shirt to kiss my stomach, a moan escaped my mouth before I was able to stop it.

"Wow Jas, just from me kissing your stomach?" Mo always had that effect on me, and he knew it. Unfortunately, he messed up bad, and I didn't think I could ever forgive him.

"I'm not going to lie; it felt good to feel your touch, and I miss you too. This was supposed to be us every day, but you messed it up. Mo, I'm in a good space now, and I can't have you interrupt that when this is not where you want to be." He looked at me and wiped the tears away, laid my head on his shoulder, and sat there with me looking out at the water.

"Jas, there is nothing I want to do more than take you home, make love to you, and erase all the pain. I know I fucked up bad and that you may never forgive me. I need you to know that, even after all that happened, I am still very much in love with you, no matter what you hear. You're the only one with my heart and the one who I want in my life now and always." He hugged me, and I started crying in his arms.

This was something I needed to do in order to move on. I needed him to tell me why he did it, but I couldn't hear it. I started wiping my eyes, stood up, and walked to my car. He walked me to my car and closed the door. I rolled the window down and allowed him to stick his head in, placing kisses on my lips.

We heard a horn blowing, and wouldn't you know; it was Lola yelling at him about being with me. I couldn't sit in the car without letting her know what it was. I opened the car door and walked to her car with Mo following.

"I told you he would never be yours the way you want him to. I suggest you get used to me being in his life, because this is happening soon." I pointed to my stomach.

"See, I let you have him, but for some reason, he misses home. Now, at first, I thought he picked you because you were pretty, or had one up on me in the bedroom, but I realized that he slept with you because I neglected him to take care of my sister. What I think you should do right now is hope and pray that I don't take him back. If that day ever comes, you need to know that you will become nonexistent in his life, because this right here will always belong to me." I told her, pointing to his heart. Now, you have a good night, and Mo, I will let you know when I get home. I got in my car and pulled off, leaving her sitting their looking stupid. The entire time, Mo was leaned up against the car smiling.

Me: Mo, we are home safe.

Mo: Thanks for texting me and letting me finally talk to you. I didn't want to hurt you, but I know that talk was what we both needed. He sent me and emoji with a tear falling, insinuating that he was crying, but I would have to see that to believe it.

Me: I think you're right. There was a weight lifted, and now, I can move on.

Mo: I don't want you to move on unless it's with me.

Me: How can I move on with you when you are still with the woman you hurt me with? You couldn't even leave her alone to fight for us, and that hurts.

Mo: Can I come see you? This is too much texting for me. I told him yes, but that he was leaving when we finished talking. I jumped in the shower, and when I came out, he was sitting on my bed. Damn, did this nigga run over here? How the hell did he get here so fast? I sat at my vanity and picked up the lotion. I was rubbing my legs when he started speaking.

"Jas, I only stayed messing around with her, because she was the only person I was fucking with before you. Does that make it right? No. I should've been fighting for you, but I never gave up, you know that. Seeing you tonight made me realize how much I can't live without you." I looked at him with his hands on his legs and looking at me, waiting to see what I was going to say.

"All I want to know is what did I do wrong to make you cheat? I gave you the best of me, and it still wasn't good enough."

"Baby, you didn't do anything wrong. I was mad at what you did at the doctor's office, and I felt like you were spending too much time with everyone else. We just got back from Virginia, and you wanted to stay at the hospital. She came over talking all this shit about why I chose you and one thing led to another. I'm sorry I hurt you like this. I swear Jas, if you take me back, I'll kill myself before I cheat on you. I need you in my life. Please, I can't take this shit." He said, now sitting in front of me, with tears coming down his eyes.

There were so many emotions going on that I started crying. He looked up to ask me if I was ok.

"No, everything is fine. I'm crying, because you said you need me, and I haven't heard you say that in a long time. I need you too, Mo, but I don't want to make a mistake taking you back. You can never hurt me like that again; I don't think I will survive it, and I think you know that."

He picked me up and laid me on the bed. I let him unwrap my towel and place kisses on my lips. I slipped my tongue in his mouth and the fire was ignited. He sucked on my neck, breast, and made his way down to Katy.

"Katy, I'm so sorry daddy neglected you. I'm here to give you what you missed." He spoke to my pussy, as I sat up on my elbows, watching him slide his tongue up and down my lips. It had been so long since I felt his touch that my pearl exploded as soon as he touched her. He sucked all my juices out, and gave me a few more body shaking orgasms.

He took all his clothes off and climbed on top of me, placing himself inside. He started off slow just the way I liked it. I was throwing it back at him, when he wanted me on top. I placed him inside and slid down slowly, looking into his eyes. He loved watching my faces and hearing my moans. I arched my back and held onto the bed, riding him back and forth.

"Baby, ride it just like that. Oh shit, yea. Just like that." He said, about to cum. "Fuck, I'm about to cum, baby. I want you to cum with me." He was massaging my clit and making me shake like crazy, as that orgasm felt like it wouldn't stop.

"Yes, Mo. I'll take you back, but on one condition." I told him, as he was smiling and kissing me all over.

"What's that baby?"

"If you ever feel neglected again, you have to tell me." I started sucking on his fingers turning him back on.

"Damn girl, you really missed me. You want to have sex again?"

"No, I want you to make love to me as only you can."

"Baby, you made me the happiest man. I'll make love to you every day all day if you want. I'm never going to hurt you again. I let him make my body do things I never knew it could.

Mo must've woke up before me, because he was gone by the time I got out of bed around ten. When I went downstairs, there were boxes everywhere and a U-Haul truck outside.

"Mo, what's going on?" I yelled out to him, because he was outside on the phone.

"Nothing, I'm moving in. I got up after you went to sleep, packed up my stuff and brought it here. I don't want you to ever feel like I'm cheating on you again. Are you mad?" He looked up at me smiling that perfect smile.

"No, baby, I'm not. I was going to ask you when I woke up, but I guess you read my mind. I'm hungry, though. Can we go to Perkins?" I asked him, while he put the last box in the house and closed the door.

"We can go wherever you want as long as we're together." When I opened the door, Mike, Jess, and Damien were standing there laughing.

"What y'all laughing at?"

"Nothing, Damien and Mike are going back and forth slapping hands. Wait, is that Mo? What are all these boxes?" Jess started asking a million questions.

"We can talk over breakfast."

Ty

Lola called me and told me everything that went down with Jas and her sisters, and I couldn't have been happier. Mo's nightmare became my new beginning for Jas, and she didn't even know it. I packed a bag to go back down to Jersey and try to win Jasmine back since she broke up with Mo. It had been over two months, and Mo was trying his hardest to win her back, but from Lola was saying, she wasn't having it. He had done the ultimate betrayal to her, and he couldn't be forgiven. Lola went back to fucking Mo whenever he called her, and she was ok with that, because Jas was out of the picture. He didn't love Jas, because he would've never gone back to fucking Lola.

I stopped by my dad's house to check on him, because I hadn't heard from him in a few days. I waited for my mom to leave, knowing she would tell my brother that I was back in town and send those niggas over. I walked in the house and saw my dad in the living room watching TV.

"Bring your ass in here, boy." He yelled out from the other room. I strolled in there after I took a beer from the fridge. I sat on the chair opposite of him.

"What up, Pop? How you been doing over?"

"Fuck all that dumb shit. What the fuck is this I hear about you shooting your brother's wife, violating some woman, and almost killing another. I mean that pussy has you acting the same as before. Now, you escaped prison time before when you did that but these are some real niggas out here gunning for you."

My dad was old school, but he wasn't clueless when it came to the streets. He had a lot of friends who had kids in the drug and murder game, so they always knew what was going on.

"I don't know, Dad. It's like she has this powerful hold over me." I took a sip of beer. My dad looked at me, I guess, trying to read me, when he started talking that bullshit,

"Listen son. Pussy is a powerful thing. The way to escape is to stay away from it. You can't go around trying to make a woman be with you, because you don't want her to be with someone else. Women have a way of using it to their advantage, especially, when they know what they're working with, but you have to know when no means no. See, in this generation of niggas growing up, y'all assume she has to give up the pussy if she's your girl, and that is far from the truth." I tried to cut him off.

"No, don't cut me off. Now, you violated that girl, not once, but twice, and you are under the assumption that she wanted it. You thought beating on her would make her stay, but instead she left. I'm not saying she didn't have feelings for you at some point, but you scarred that woman, and now you have niggas looking for you. I know they found you once and didn't kill you, and that was probably because they had other plans for you. I don't want to lose a son, but I think you need to take them serious and get the fuck out of dodge." He spoke with great concern, and I listened, but I wasn't leaving without Jas.

"I hear you, dad, but I'm good. I'm meeting with Jas later, and this will all be behind us soon enough."

"Ok, I spoke my peace, and I wish you weren't so hardheaded, but that's your life you playing Russian roulette with."

"Let me ask you a question son. Does this woman know she's going to meet with you?"

I stood up, patted my dad on the shoulder, and told him he worried too much. I walked out, got in my car, and went on Jess' page to see if she posted anything about where she was going. I had no idea where she would, be but when I scrolled IG, and she posted that she wanted some seafood, and I remembered the only place that she loved, besides the Outback, and that was where I was headed.

I got to Red Lobster looking for Jas' car, but I didn't see it right away. After looking on the other side of the parking lot, I found it. I hopped out the car, checked my clothes, and walked in. It was the dinner rush, and I knew that she wouldn't recognize me right away, so I sat at the bar waiting for my plan to kick in. I looked back and saw Jas give her order to the waitress, when some man sat in the booth with her. I could tell that she didn't want any company by the way she looked. I could hear her getting loud with the guy and shit, and since she wasn't with Mo, I will be that knight and shining armor today.

"Excuse me my man. Can I help you?" When Jas saw me, she looked around like she was scared but didn't move.

"Mind your business, yo'. This doesn't concern you at all."

"This is my girl, and I'm going to ask you to back away from our table." I told him, lifting my shirt to show him the 9mm tucked in my waist. He backed away from the table, and I reached down to give Jas a kiss on the cheek. She pulled away, and I was ok with that, because she had to get used to me again.

"Do you mind if I take a seat?" I was shocked when she nodded her head yes. I excused myself to use the bathroom before I sat down with her and ran into the guy that was just bothering her.

"Yo', my man. Thanks for doing that. Here's the two hundred I promised." I patted him on the back and walked into the bathroom. This shit went a lot smoother than I thought it would. I washed my hands, threw the paper towel in the garbage, and walked back to the table. I took a seat and just stared at how beautiful she was. I mean, she did gain a little weight, but it was in all the right places. It was May, and she was wearing a maxi dress with a small jean jacket around her arms. Her hair was in a ponytail, and she had no makeup on.

"So, how have you been Jas?" I asked her, shooing the waitress away that came to see if I wanted to order. I wanted her all to myself with no interruptions.

"I'm doing good, Ty. I mean, Mo cheated on me. The chic sent me all the videos and pictures, which crushed me. It was hard getting over that, but I was strong enough to. From what I hear, they're still a couple, and that's fine, because it's going to be about me and her." I was at a loss for words, because in all the talking with Lola, she never told me that Jas was pregnant.

"Oh, wow. I had no idea you were expecting. Congratulations. Even though I wish that that was our baby. That could've been our baby if that nigga would've cheated sooner. We could be living our happily ever after right now, but he wouldn't leave you alone. That's ok; I'll help you raise the baby if you want."

"Thanks Ty, but I think we'll manage, and I'm sure that I'll be going through a lot of shit with him over her. But how have you been?"

"I'm good. I went back home to Maryland to get my shit together. I have changed so much, and I would love to start over with you."

"Wow. You're just going to jump right in with that shit, huh?"

"I just feel like we got off to a rough start because of that nigga, but now that he's out of the picture, I think we should try again. I don't care that you got pregnant; I still want to be with you. Who knows, after you drop this load, I could fill you up again with a mini me."

She had the prettiest smile, and I missed hearing her laugh. We stayed there for about an hour talking when her phone started ringing and her screen popped up showing Mo's name.

"I swear, I need to get my phone number changed." She pouted, hitting the decline button on her phone.

"I better get out of here. I have some work to catch up on, but it was good seeing you Ty. She went to leave the money, but I told her that I had it. I walked out with her to her car and asked if we could meet up again. I gave her my new cell and told her to call me when she was free. I would be in town for another week, and I was going to try my best to win her over. I waved, as she pulled off, then left myself.

Mike

It was like somebody snatched a piece of my soul when I saw Jess lying in that hospital bed like that. I knew that that nigga Ty did it just from the text I received from him and his time was ticking. I loved how Ms. Gomez went in on my mom, because it kept me from doing it. Unfortunately, my mom did the ultimate betrayal by letting my ex stay in her house, not telling me, then saying that Jess was no longer needed in so many words.

I saw Mo look down at his phone, then look straight up at Jas, like something was about to kick off. Before I knew it, there was fucking chaos all in Jess' room. Someone sent a video to everybody's phone of Mo fucking this chic. I snatched Jess' phone out her hand, because she did not need to see my brother's dick. Jas was devastated, and now, I could see what women go through when a man cheats. I vowed never to do that shit to Jess, no matter how hard it was. That was why I passed up Maria's ass, and I was glad that I did, or I would be going through the same shit.

I heard everything that went down after they left the hospital, from them whipping Lola's ass, to going to threaten Mo. I cursed Mo's ass out over that shit, because we had known them for over fifteen years, and even though they weren't together, she wasn't a random chic. I also asked him why he was still fucking Lola if he was trying to win Jas back. His dumb ass just said he didn't know.

Jess got released two weeks after the accident but was placed on strict bed rest. Her mom and I waited on her hand and foot, and the girls came over almost every day to sit with her. Jess was so carefree about the whole situation, but I was furious and couldn't wait to get that nigga. The girls brought some weed and drinks over one day, and Jess must've had a little too much.

I got home from the bar, when my sisters were leaving the house fucked up with Jas as the designated driver. I gave each one of them a hug and rubbed Jas' stomach. She was so happy to be pregnant, and I couldn't blame her. I walked up the stairs, and Jess was laid out on the couch, watching one of Kevin Hart's comedy specials and cracking up. I figured that that must've been why those fools were laughing so hard. I lifted her up, sitting down, and put her head on my lap.

"Hey baby. I missed you. How was your day?" She asked me, rolling her back, looking straight at me. I reached down and kissed her lips.

"It was ok. I missed you, too, but I always miss you as soon as I walk out the door."

She reached her arms up, pulled my face down, and kissed me, causing my dick to get hard. It had been over two months since she had her accident, and I was ready to fuck, but I would never cheat on her. I just had to wait for her to be ready and tonight was that night. We started kissing more intense, when she rolled over on her stomach and told me to pull my pants and boxers down.

I wanted this so bad that I couldn't get them down fast enough. She went up and down on my dick with her mouth keeping him nice and moist just the way she knew I liked it. She had me cumming in two minutes flat before waking him up again. She told me that she wanted to see how many times she could make me bust this way like I do for her. I'm telling you, her head game was so official that, after the fourth time, I came so hard that I had to sit her up.

I know she still moves in slow motion, so I pulled her pajama pants down and stuck my tongue directly on her pearl, causing her to jump. I felt her hand on my head, and when I looked up, she was getting so much pleasure that her body began to shake. I had her climbing the couch trying to get away from this mouth on her clit, when her entire body went limp after that first orgasm. I wiped my mouth with the back of my hand and stuck my fingers inside finding her g-spot right away. Her juices escaped her, before she could catch her breath.

I picked her up and carried her to the bedroom. She took my dick, slid him in her pussy, and tensed up right away.

"Baby, it's ok, we can wait. You gave me more than enough for a while tonight." I whispered in her ear. She was not trying to hear that shit, as she put her finger over my mouth.

"I want to feel you inside me. Please give me what I want." She begged me, and I forced him in, making her scream out in pain. She dug so hard in my back, breaking my skin, but it was well worth it.

Once she got used to me, it was like old times again. I laid her on her back and threw her legs over my shoulder. Her pussy was so wet that I came right away. She couldn't get on top or all fours, yet, because her legs were still healing. I turned her on the side and fucked her nice and rough like she wanted it.

"Baby, I want to do a 69 with you." I laid her on top of me, and tore that pussy up. I had to stop when she took my balls in her mouth.

"Oh shit, Jess." I yelled out to her.

"Who does this book belong to always and forever?" She put him back in her mouth, and I had to say it.

"Jess, this is your dick. Oh shit, Jess. Fuck, I'm cumming." I came so hard, my toes started curling like Eddie Murphy's in the movie Boomerang. I never came like that before, and I was glad that she was the one that did it. I had to finish giving her what she needed. I had her squirting all over my face and screaming for me to stop; she couldn't take any more. She rolled off me, and I moved down to the other end of the bed with her.

"I needed that baby. Thank you." I told her, kissing her forehead.

"You're welcome. Anytime, anyplace for you." She said, cuddling up closer to me. "Mike, if you ever feel neglected, please tell me. That's what Mo told Jas was the reason for cheating. I don't ever want you to think I'm too busy to give you what you deserve." I rolled her over and looked her into the eyes.

"You never have to worry about that. I know we are twins, but I'm not Mo. Shit, I was shocked he did that myself, but he made that choice. I will never risk losing you over some ass. Plus, I doubt anyone can make me nut four times in a row off of her head game, or have me saying her name like you do. There's nothing out there I need that I can't get right here. Please know that. "

"Let's make some more twins, baby." She started playing with her pussy, calling out for me, and I had no choice but to take what she was offering. We made love all through the night, and I made sure to shoot all my babies in her. I wanted her to have all my kids even if that meant we had to fuck every day. I was getting her pregnant again.

Jess wanted to see my sisters, so we took a drive over there the next day to see who was there. I was shocked to see, what looked like, boxes all over Jas's floor, and Mo walking down the steps. When Jess asked her what was up, she just told her we would talk about it over breakfast.

Alicia

"Jas, you did great in there. Are you ok? I know it was hard sitting across from him after everything that went down, but this is the only way. Even though you screamed Mo's name out, you threw that pussy on his ass, and now, he doen't know what to do with himself. Hey, did y'all make a video? Maybe, we can let Mo watch that shit to see how he likes it." I was looking at Mo, who was mad as hell that I brought that shit up.

"Girl, stop. You always starting shit, but I never have to worry when you or Candace are around. I love y'all, but it was hard acting like I was ok with everything that had happened. Just looking at him was pissing me off, but I kept my cool." Jas said.

"Well, what's the next move? I know it may feel like we're using you Jas, but you know it's too many of us for him to hurt you. He got away with that shit in the beginning, because he, basically, kidnapped you, but that will never happen again. Even when you think we're not around, just know that someone is always watching you." Mike said, giving her a hug.

"Yo', Mo, pass that shit." I noticed him, making these evil eyes at me, but I didn't give a fuck. He hurt Jas to her core, and for that, I will always look at him sideways.

"Alicia, let me talk to you for a minute." Mo asked me, getting up from the chair and walking out the door. I followed his ass and sat on the porch next to him.

"Listen, I know what I did to Jas was fucked up, and I still wake up every day feeling like shit, knowing that I can't erase that from her memory. You think I don't know that she worries that I will do it, again, but I'm not. That's why the same day she took me back, I moved in hours later to prove that I was serious. I love that woman with all my heart and soul and vowed that I would never allow another woman to come between us. I know that, when one of y'all hurt, you all do, and I can respect that. I don't want us being mad at each other over what happened. You my dog; my sister, too, and I hate that we're acting like this with one another."

"I love you, too, bro, and I'm shocked you even said anything instead of fucking me up like you would've done before. Remember, we would go blow for blow back in the day. I missed talking to you, and this is the first time we smoked together in a long time. Let's go back in before they smoke all our shit. You know we the only ones that paid for that shit today." I gave him a hug and walked back inside the house. Jas looked at us trying to figure out what that was about, and we just shrugged our shoulders. I know one of us will tell her later, but right now, we needed to talk about what was next.

There was a knock at the door, and Mike got up to answer it, because he said he was waiting on someone. Me, Jess, and

Candace all dropped our mouths, when she walked in the house with another guy. This woman was drop dead gorgeous and resembled Jas in so many ways. Mike look at us shaking his head, because he knew we wanted to know who the fuck she was.

"Hello everyone. She walked around and introduced herself and her husband. Jess was sitting on Mike's lap when she walked over.

"You must be Jessica. Mike, this is the woman you were rushing home to?" She gave her apologies for the accident. Jas walked to the bathroom when she walked in, but her eyes almost popped out her head when RiRi looked at her.

"Mo, I thought you were lying when you said we resembled. Oh, my God, it's almost like looking in a mirror. Jas, I am happy to finally meet you." She gave Jas a hug and apologized for not handling the situation sooner, so that it didn't happen to any other woman.

"Hey." Cornell said, giving her a kiss on the cheek.

"Oh, hell no. Hello, I'm Alicia, and this is Candace, Jas's other sister. Who the fuck are you coming in here acting like you know them?"

"Baby, calm down. Give her a minute to explain herself before you start going off. Not everybody is an enemy, damn." Cornell said, pulling me back.

"Wow, Cornell you have a live one, huh? I like that. She is the same way I am over him, so I'm not offended. I think she and I are just alike."

Once she told us all who she was, I remembered exactly who she was. Her husband was a lieutenant for the FBI, but he was gangsta as hell. Mo sparked another blunt, and he asked to puff with us. We were shocked, but I guess even cops needed to stay calm. I asked her what she was doing here, and she started talking until she got to the part of what happened to her. She didn't want to speak on it too much, but Jas went and sat by her.

"I didn't want to talk about it, either. It was even harder when I spoke on it, because I did it in front of all my family, and I denied the whole thing at first, but as I told the story, I felt a weight being lifted, and it made me stronger knowing that he didn't win. If you don't want to talk in front of everyone, we can go outside if you want." Jas told her, but she stayed and said she trusted everyone in the room. She felt like her business was all over the news, so it wasn't a secret anyway. I felt bad for the way I snapped on her when she first got there, so I apologized to her.

"Ok, so why don't we just kill this motherfucker now? I mean, what are we waiting for? I'm down, but I need to do some things to him first for shooting me." I yelled out, and Cornell told me to sit my ass down.

"Look, the only person he trust right now is Jas. He has become obsessed with her so bad that we made him think he paid a guy $200 to do something, when we set that whole shit up ourselves. He gave her his new number and said that he would be in town for another week, so we need to get this shit done and over with. Jas, you know we all love you, and if this is not something you want to do, then it's ok, we can go another route."

"No, it's ok. As long as I know all of you guys will be somewhere close, and it won't affect me or my baby, I'll do it."

"Baby, I don't know that I feel comfortable with you going around him again. I mean Red Lobster, yea. It's always crowded there, and he can't do anything, but when you talk about meeting up with him at a certain spot, I'm not down with that shit."

"Ok, look. When she tells him to meet her, it doesn't have to be a room or anything like that. We will keep you guys out in the open as much as possible." I said to her.

"Right now, I want you to text him and say you're not feeling well, and that you will catch him the next time he's in town. The reason I think we should wait is, because he will have to text Jas a bit before he will really trust her again. We have to let him continue thinking that she and Mo aren't together. Jas, you may not like it, but he will have to stay in touch with Lola. We have to make everything as normal as possible." I said, knowing that shit was making Jas uncomfortable, but if we wanted this nigga out of our life, we had to do it.

"My dad is going in for surgery next month, and Ty told him he would be down for it. We could use that time to get everything in order." Cornell was rubbing my back trying to get me to calm down.

"Wait, Jas' baby shower is next month. When is your dad's surgery?" I asked my husband.

"It's not until the 28th, and the shower is the 16th, so we have more than enough time after that to focus."

"Would you like to attend the shower?"

"Sure, if Jas and Mo don't mind, I would love to come." She said, looking at them, as they nodded their heads yes.

"Well, alrighty, then. Let's get this shit started." I said, jumping up to run to the bathroom.

Candace

It was Jasmine's baby shower, and I had so much to do. I got Malik and Alicia running around with me to help out, but I don't know why Jas agreed to let Mo's mom throw the shower, when she know damn well she don't care for her. I know that that was going to be the grandmother, and all, but she is such a bitch. She was lucky she wasn't related to my kids, because she would get the major curse out every damn day.

"Come on, Malika. Alicia's outside blowing the horn." I yelled up the steps, when my daughter came down, half-dressed, with small ass shorts, and a half shirt.

"Oh, hell no. Take your ass back upstairs and change. And hurry your ass up."

"Ms. D, we'll be back to pick you and the rest of the kids up when we're finished setting up. Please don't get the kids ready until an hour before the party. I want them clean until we get there, and then they can tear shit up." I told her, walking out the door, getting ready to leave Malika's ass. She came down the steps fully dressed with her earpiece in, probably, so she could ignore me, but I didn't give a fuck.

We went from store to store getting balloons and decorations, and Alicia got her the two-in-one jogging stroller that she wanted. I got her an expensive ass swing that she wanted. We got to Ms. Watson's house, and she had that shit smelling good as hell with all the food she was cooking. We walked in the house and saw collard greens, baked macaroni and cheese, ox tails, cabbage, sausage and peppers, baked beans, pulled pork, and the list goes on and on.

As we were walking to the back, the DJ knocked on the door asking where to set up. Malika took him outside and pointed to where we told her he could. I walked outside, and Mo had a huge tent put in the back with floors and the sides hung down just in case it rained. There were tons of tables and chairs that we had to decorate with tablecloths and party favors.

We decorated Jasmine's chair with a few balloons and a chair cover, and Malika thought it would be cute to put pink shower bows around her chair. We decorated another table for all the candy, cupcakes, and any baby gifts that came. The other few tables had racks and sternos set up for the food. The backyard looked so pretty that I knew that Jasmine was going to cry when she saw it, along with the surprise that I had coming for her. It was an hour before the shower was to start, so Alicia dropped us off to get changed. I was so glad that Ms. D had the kids ready, so that Malika and I could get ready and leave.

We got to the shower before any guest arrived to make sure all the food was out and everything was ready. The first guests to arrive were the employees that worked with us, and after that, people just started flowing in. Jess and Mike walked in holding hands with Damien in Mike's other arm. You could tell that he was nervous from all the people there, as he was clinging to him. When Damien saw Malika, he reached out for her, and she started smiling and talking baby talk, taking him from Mike. Those two formed a bond when they first met, and we all loved it, but Malika had always been great with kids, because of her siblings.

Alicia, Cornell, Ms. Leslie, and their daughter walked up holding a pan of baked ziti that his mom made. Cornell walked it back and took Mike with him to grab a beer. Jessica excused herself to go into the bathroom, when Jas and Mo walked up. After all the shit they been through, you couldn't tell that they didn't love each other. She and Mo gave me a big hug for setting it all up. We all walked in the backyard to get the shower started, and we sat at the same table, but when I looked around, everyone was eating, except Jess. I leaned over to find out what was up. Alicia looked at me and shrugged her shoulders, because she was throwing down on some greens.

"Girl, why aren't you eating? It's mad food out there." I saw her look at Mike, who was feeding Damien some macaroni and cheese. I looked at both of them like what? Shit I didn't know if something was wrong with the food or what.

"Every time I eat, it comes back up. I don't really feel like vomiting at Jas' shower. I will try and eat later." I looked at her, then back at Mike.

"Bitch, you pregnant?" I said that shit so loud that I didn't realize it until everybody at the table looked at her for the answer. She was so fucking scary that she just put her head in Mike's arm.

"Damn, Candace, you ask too many questions sometimes." Mike said, before asking Jess if she wanted to say something or not. She looked at everybody staring at her and nodded her head yes. Everybody at the table was so happy for her after what she went through, and Jas wobbled out her seat and gave her a big hug.

"I fucking knew it. You used to want to go out to eat with me every few days, and then when I called, you kept saying you weren't feeling well. Girl, why didn't you say something?" She asked her.

"I was going to tell everybody tomorrow." She said, as Mike put his arms around her and kissed her. Damien climbed on Mike's lap and gave Jess a kiss on the mouth just like Mike did, and then said, "No kiss, mommy. Only me." We all started cracking up. He was really becoming a talker, now, I guess from being around so many kids in daycare and us.

"Jess, you are our sister, now, and how many times we told you there are no secrets? I know you are big on family, but you need to open up to us if you expect us to know you better. Shit, Damien is more opened up to us than you are." I said, making everybody laugh again. My phone started vibrating, which let me know the surprise was on it's way.

After we ate, Jas and Mo opened all the gifts with the help of my two little ones, Damien and Leslie. The kids just loved ripping the paper off and throwing it. I had to yell at their asses a few times, because paper was everywhere. It was getting late, and the party was starting to wind down. The guys were out in the back when the woman, her husband, and the surprise walked in. Jasmine was sitting at the table with Ms. D, Ms. Watson, Ms. Gomez and all of us, when she looked up and started crying hysterically. One of the kids ran out and got Mo, because no one knew what happened.

"Baby, what's wrong?" He asked her, as she stood up walking towards the other woman.

"Nothing is wrong; that's my mother." She told him, walking to give her a hug. Mo was standing there wondering how she was able to make it but saw who was standing next to her and nodded.

Jasmine

It was the day of my baby shower, which meant it was almost time to deal with Ty once and for all shortly after. Ty and I had been texting back and forth for the past month, and I was starting to get aggravated doing it. He wanted us to meet at a hotel when he came into town, talking about he wanted privacy. I refused to be caught alone with that man again. Right before the shower, he sent me a text asking to send him pictures of my pussy, because he missed it and needed to jerk off. I shut my phone off, not wanting to deal with him for the rest of the day.

Things weren't any better with Mo's ass and Lola either. He was sending her text messages every other day just asking how she was doing. She wanted to know why he moved back in with his mom, because she couldn't come see him there. She knew his mom couldn't stand her ass and wouldn't even let her on the property. Then, she started talking about his dick and how she missed sucking it and all the positions he would fuck her in.

He doesn't know I saw those messages, but he didn't respond when she sent those. She even sent him the video that she had that she sent me trying to make him reminisce. I deleted that shit as soon as it came through. I kept telling myself that it wouldn't be too much longer, but it was killing me. She sent one today, too, about the shower, because Candace posted it on IG, and she wanted to know why he was going if we weren't together.

"Babe, I don't feel like going. Let's stay home and make love all night." I told him, watching him dry off with the towel, licking my lips.

"Hell no, Jas. We fucked all day, and my dick is tired, so stop looking at it like that. Get dressed, so we can go."

I put on a long, black maxi skirt, a camisole shirt, and some black Michael Kors loafers. I pulled my hair up, put on earrings, a small amount of lip gloss, and walked out the door.

"Damn girl, no matter what you wear, you are still beautiful. The way your titties look in that shirt makes me want to breastfeed."

"Oh no, bro. You won't breastfeed off of these until I can suck on that bottle in between your legs." He got in the driver's seat, looking at me like he was getting ready to say something, but I beat him to it.

"That's what your ass gets. You should've taken it when I was giving it out. Now, you have to wait, but I love you." I gave him a kiss on the lips, and he drove off.

We pulled up to his moms, and there were a ton of cars out there, but Candace saved us a spot close, so I didn't have to walk that far. Mo helped me get out the truck and whispered in my ear.

"I'm going to get your ass back. Just wait until Katy wants me to talk to her again."

My sisters decorated the shower so nicely, and there was so much food. Candace and Alicia had everybody playing these baby games. I think Malika won a gift that she couldn't keep, because it was two bottles of wine. A few other people won some gifts as well. We found out Jess was pregnant, again, by Mike, and I was so happy for her. I watched her cry her eyes out when we finally told her she lost the babies. And then, to watch me still pregnant was rough, but it worked out for her in the end, and I was so happy that I'd be an aunty again.

Everyone was still sitting at the table with me when my mom walked in. I was crying so hard that the kids went to get Mo who thought something had happened. I gave her the biggest hug ever, and Ms. D was crying, because her and my mom were best friends before she went to jail for killing my father.

"Mom, how did you get out? Candace, did you know mom was out?" By this time all the guys had walked in, Alicia ran over kissing her and crying when she saw her. My mom had raised her when her dad died. We were teenagers when her mom died and her dad said she was always with us anyway so she may as well live there. He passed away from Cancer not too long after, leaving her with millions that I was not sure she even told her husband about yet.

She got hugs from Darrell, Mike, and Mo, when she smacked Mo with her cane on his arm. Alicia introduced her to Cornell, his mom and their daughter. It was like a family reunion, and it was the best surprise ever.

"Now, Jasmine Marie Smith, what is this I hear about you letting some man beat and violate you? Didn't you learn anything from what you saw your father do to me? I know what happened to you is partly my fault. I stayed with your father so many years, and you were the only one who witnessed it all. Candace and Alicia were always talking about these three niggas right here, and he was scared that they would tell and get them to kill him. I never meant for you to see all that and keep it a secret. Maybe, if you would've told your sisters, I wouldn't have went through extreme measures to save us." She said, as I sat there crying with flashbacks of the beatings. He would always tell my mom that it was her fault, because she did something wrong. If she would've just did it right, then he wouldn't hit her.

"Mom, he was bigger than me, and I couldn't find the strength to fight back until recently. I been through so much stuff, and you didn't want any of us coming to see you or writing to you. You kept saying that we don't need to see the inside of a prison; not even to visit. I didn't have anyone but Ms. D, and she was the mom for you, and I appreciate everything she did for me, but I needed you. I still need you." I said to her, making my sisters cry.

"Well, I'm not sure who this woman is, but they pulled some strings after you met them to get me here. I got a year left off a 12-year bid, but he said, if you help them, I can get right out. Now, Jasmine, I know this is your shower and that you may not want to talk about it here, but this FBI guy here and his wife have been watching over you since she left Virginia.

You girls don't know, but I had him keeping y'all safe for some years now. I didn't know the woman he was married to had ties to you, because of that nigga. This man right here is Mario, and he is your cousin on our dad's side. His mom was your dad's sister, and you never met him, because he was nine or ten when I killed your dad, and his mom refused to allow him any contact with you.

"Wait a minute. You are Aunt Rosie's son, Mario, who used to live in Red Bank?" Alicia asked, remembering him from when her dad used to take her over there. He looked at us and nodded his head yes.

"Oh shit, so we got a FED in the family?" Alicia's crazy ass said, cracking up. He walked up to me and handed me a present for the baby. When I pulled the box open, it was a baby bangle that said, "For an angel." I gave him and his wife a kiss on the cheek, thanking them for the expensive gift and asked them how long was they staying.

"He got my mom home on some furlough shit, so she was staying with me, and Mo for the night. Of course, Candace already copped a squat at my house, and so did Alicia, which meant my house would be packed. We sat around for a few more hours until the kids got tired. Mo took all the presents in the house and said that we would be back tomorrow to pick them up.

When we got back to the house, my mom went in on Mo about cheating and how he allowed a woman to record his ass fucking and taking pictures. I don't know why, but a light went off, when I never asked how she was able to get that. She had to be working with someone, but who was it. I had to run that by Mo, even though it didn't excuse his ass for what he did.

We were all exhausted and went to bed after one, getting ready to prepare for this shit with Ty. Everybody got a text from Mike saying that, since tomorrow was Sunday, and my mom was home, we should go out to dinner.

Mike

Jess had been throwing up for the past three weeks, and she kept claiming that she had some flu, at first, but we found out that her ass was pregnant. She didn't want to tell anyone until tomorrow because of the baby shower, because she didn't want to take the shine away from Jas. That was why I loved her; she was so considerate of other people, but I had to get her to stop being so damn scary.

When we got there, I watched her run into the bathroom to throw up. This baby was kicking her ass more than the last two. I bet it was a boy wreaking havoc in her stomach, and that was a good thing, because that meant that he would come out swinging.

Candace's ass blew Jess' secret by screaming out she was pregnant, because she wasn't eating. I swear, Candace never thinks before she screams shit out. Jess acted all shy like she didn't know that, with all the fucking that we were doing, this was going to happen. I gave her a kiss and lil' man started smacking my mouth telling me not to kiss her. I love that lil' boy, and I couldn't wait to marry his mom.

The shower ended up being fun, and when Jas' mom walked in, I knew that she was going to lose it. She started crying, kissing, and hugging on her. Shit, we found out her cousin was the FED dude that came with the RiRi. I damn sure didn't know her dad was whooping her mom's ass like that. I knew the stories, but when that shit happened, none of the girls ever wanted to talk about it. No wonder she was giving that nigga Ty passes after he beat her ass. She probably thought that shit was normal, but his days were numbered. I wanted to take everybody to dinner, so I sent a group text out to everyone to meet at The Four Seasons restaurant at six. I chose that time, because the kids were going to be hungry around that time.

"Come on, Jess. Me, your mom, and Damien are going out to the car."

"Are you ready?" Ms. Gomez asked, when she got into the back with Damien.

"As ready as I'm going to be." I was nervous, as hell, but it had to be done. Jess would probably be mad, but she'll be all right. I blew the horn, and Jess walked out wearing a light blue pants romper with some silver sandals, no makeup, and she had this glow about her, probably, from being pregnant. She hopped in the front seat, kissed me, and we left.

We got there around 6:15, when Candace and Alicia started asking how I set it up and why we were late. I pointed at Jess' ass. She looked down and hit me in my arm for telling that it was her fault. Everyone was there, including my mom, all the other moms, the kids, my brothers, Maria, my other son, Devon, and it just so happened that Damien's dad was there with that same chic from the bar. They must be making a relationship out of that shit they got going on.

I looked at Jess talking to my sisters and looked at Damien's dad, who walked over and told Jess that he wanted him to sit with them. She didn't pay it no mind, nodding her head ok and continuing on with her conversation with the girls. I looked at her mom, took a deep breath, and walked over to where Jess was sitting. Everyone was already aware of what was happening, so when I called Jess' name it got very quiet, besides the other people that wasn't with us. When she turned around, I was down on one knee in front of her. She started crying, as I started speaking.

"Jess, we have been together now for over six months, and you're all I think about when I wake up and when I go to sleep at night. I have been around many females, but none completes me like you do. Since you came into my life, I've become a better man because of you. When I thought I lost you at my house, I couldn't see myself without you and wanted to knock your door down, kidnap you, and make love to you until you took me back. There is no other woman in this world that loves me like you do. When you say you're glad your ex fucked up, because you found me, I see it the other way around. If he hadn't fucked up, I would've never met you. I knew that, after we first made love, you were the one for me. I feel like we were meant to be together, and I will never find another woman to make me feel the way you do.

There is no other woman that I want to carry my babies but you. I promise never to hurt you or make you cry. I want

173

to know if you'll marry me?" I asked, as Devon walked over with Damien and handed me a blue Tiffany's box. I took the five-carat yellow diamond out the box and put it on her finger. She pulled me close, said yes, and kissed me so passionately.

My sisters and all our moms were in tears, as everyone started clapping; even the people we didn't know. Mo recorded it all for me, so we could watch it later. I knew her ass was going to be hysterical. Devon gave Jess a hug and kissed her on the cheek.

Damien's dad came over to give me a hug.

"The best man has won, and I'm happy it was you. I appreciate all the help you give her with Damien, and I couldn't ask for a better man to help raise him." Damien picked up his sippy cup and laid back on my chest watching everybody.

Maria even walked up to Jess and gave her hug.

"Shit, I was with him for a few years, and he never proposed, but you locked him down in less than a year. Congratulations. I really mean that."

Jess got up and sat on my lap.

"Yup, that's this fire in between my legs that locked it down." I couldn't do shit but laugh as Jess, Candace, and Alicia walked over.

"That's right, Maria, so what does that tell you?"

"Alicia, that is so not nice. That's still my other son's mother." Jess said, watching Maria walk away pissed. She knew that Alicia couldn't stand her and that that would never go away.

"Let me see that ring bitch. I'm posting this shit right now on IG." Candace said, taking her hand. I have to say that that rock looked good on her finger. I had her take a picture of Jess, the boys, and me, so I could post it. I captioned it, *She said yes. This is my wife now, so hands off.* I tagged her in the photo. We sat there for a while and let everyone say Congratulations. When my mom walked up to Jess, everybody got real quiet.

"I'm happy that Mike chose you to be his wife. I hope we can start over one day, but until then, call me if you need anything. You have made my son a better man, and because of that, I will always love you." My mom said. Jess stood up and gave which made her cry.

The guys and I were talking at the car when Jess started yelling for Mo to come, because Jas's water broke. Everybody went running over when Jess ran over to her ex's car and asked him to come help. He stayed with Jas until the EMT's came. Jas welcomed a six pound, twelve ounce baby girl named Harmony Marie Watson. She had the smallest hands I'd ever seen. When Jess held her, all I could do was think about how she would look holding our baby. This woman had me feeling ways and doing things I never thought I would. I guess that was why she was going to be my wife. We let Damien go with his dad, dropped her mom off, and made love all night long.

Tina Jenkins

Ty

I was still waiting for Jas to send me some naked pictures of herself when I got a call from my mom saying my pops was in the hospital. He said that he had a fever and was coughing up blood. I made a reservation at the Marriott Hotel for a week just so I could be close. I walked in the hospital and ran straight into Mike's girl working at the front desk. I knew that her and Mike were getting married, because Lola sent me a picture of them yesterday. I must say the diamond was big as hell. She looked up and had the prettiest face I saw next to Jas. I didn't pay her no mind the last time, because I was set on hurting her for Mike. I walked up to the desk to play it off so that I could get my dad's room number, knowing my mom gave it to me.

"Hey. You are beautiful, do you know that?" I told her, watching the smile creep on her face.

"Thanks. You're not too bad looking yourself." I asked her for my dad's information and asked if she was married. When she said no, why? I was shocked that she even answered.

"I don't know. I was thinking we could go out for a drink after work. That's if your man don't mind." I said, pointing to her ring.

"Never mind that, no one said I couldn't have friend's right, so if you really want to get that drink after work, I'll be here until seven."

"Oh, word? Ok, give me some time to check on my dad, but let me get your number just in case you leave before I get back." She gave me her number without thinking twice. I didn't know what Mike did, but I was fucking that bitch, and I was going to do him like I did Mo. She was no Jas, but I'd still fuck her, and then, I would have had both of their women. Whew! My plan is falling into place faster than I thought.

I stayed in the room with my dad longer than I thought. By the time I realized what time it was, it was after eight o' clock. I walked out, hopped in my car, and ran to the closest convenience store to grab a prepaid phone. I went back to my hotel, set the phone up, and text Jessica. I'm not stupid. If he looked through her phone, he wasn't going to find my number. I started texting her to see if she was going to come out for that drink.

Me: Hey you. Can you still get out for that drink tonight?

I sat the phone down to order some room service. I was starving, and I didn't feel like eating at that hospital cafeteria.

Jessica: Not tonight. My man is going out with his boys tomorrow, so it will be easier for me to get out. Where do you want to meet up?

Me: There's a new club in Brick called Mansions. We would be out of town and away from everyone.

Jessica: Ok, text me the address, tomorrow, and I will meet you there around ten, if that's ok.

Me: Ok, I'll hit you up tomorrow, and it's more of an upscale club.

Jessica: Good. I love dressing up. I'm going to shop for something sexy.

Me: Mmmmm sounds good to me. Have a good night.

Jessica: See you tomorrow. Make sure I'm not the only one dressed up.

Me: Never. I have something special to wear just for you.

Jessica: Ok, I'll see you tomorrow.

After she and I finished texting, I couldn't help but to think about Jas and us meeting up. I refused to allow Mo to win Jas from me. That was my soul mate, and he was going to give her up, whether he wanted to, or not.

My food came, and I ate that shit like it was my last meal. I got in the shower and picked out what I was wearing tomorrow night. I bought extra clothes for me and Jas to go out, but I could always go shopping if I needed to. I wondered what my brother was doing, but I'd be damned if I went by there. I may have to kill his wife for real this time.

I woke up the next day and went to visit my dad again. He was feeling a little better when my mom walked in asking what I was doing there.

"This is my dad. What do you mean what am I doing here? Shit, you called me." I said, now getting aggravated with her.

"I only called for him. I didn't expect your ass to come here. You know them niggas got a hit out on your ass, and you taking chances coming back to town."

"Ain't nobody thinking about those niggas. Y'all spending too much time on worrying about if they're going to catch me."

"Well, say what you want, but I don't think it's a game. Especially, after what they're saying you did to that other girl. I think it was Mike's girlfriend. They're saying you ran her over, making her lose the twins that she was pregnant with. And from what I hear, he is ten times worse than Mo, so I wouldn't take that shit lightly.

"Ok, Ma. Damn. I'm not here for all that. I am only staying for a week, so I'll know he's all right. Shit, what you doing here anyway? Dad can't stand your ass. He only has you here so he doesn't die alone." I said to her, watching her face drop, when she looked at my dad.

"Is this true? Is that the only reason you asked me to move back here?" He just looked at me, shaking his head and trying to speak.

"You are one foul ass man. Your momma didn't raise you to treat woman like that, and why you sitting here hurting your mother?" He was coughing the whole time.

"Man, I'm out of here." I said, walking out the door, running straight into that guy that looked like my ex's new husband. I was sure that that wasn't him, because he would've noticed me from the trial. Oh well; if it was, his punk ass didn't say or do shit. I went back to the room and laid down. I must've dozed off, because when I looked up, it was eight o' clock. I jumped up, remembering my date with Jessica and sent her a text of the address that and said that I would be there by ten. It was 9:45, and I sat out in my car waiting for Jessica to show up. I waited when I saw her pull up to the Valet to be sure she was alone.

I walked into the club ten minutes later, when I was sure no one followed her. She was rocking a white mini dress, gold laced up heels, light makeup and no engagement ring.

"Hey. I must say, you are stunning. I am happy that your man didn't see you dressed like this, because I know he wouldn't let you out like this." I whispered in her ear, causing her to jump and look.

"You scared me. You look mighty handsome yourself. She looked me up and down.

"Have you ordered yet?" When she said, no, I flagged the waiter over. She ordered some Apple martinis, and I asked for two shots of Jack Daniels.

"So, what's up with you? Are you from around here?" I told her, I was in town for my dad and trying to take back something that was stolen from me.

"Sounds like a woman if you ask me."

"Something like that, but I hope that doesn't affect us being friends. I won't tell if you don't." I told her, watching her put the drink down and grab my hand to go dancing. We stayed out there for a few songs when she excused herself to use the ladies' room. I ordered her a drink, and when no one was looking, I put a molly pill inside. I stirred it around a little before she got back.

"I took the liberty of ordering you a new drink. You can never be too careful leaving your drinks around.

"You're right. Thanks." We talked and danced some more, when I noticed her starting to get groggy. She was slurring at her words and staggering. I saw her eyes get real big, when some dude walked up to speak.

"Hey Jess. Ugh what's up?" He asked her, clearly trying to figure out why she was there with some man.

'Oh, nothing. I'm just here wiiithhh mmmyyy friend. Oh shit, I don't even think you told me your name. What is your name?"

"I got this my man. She's with me. I'll make sure to get her home safe." I saw him, watching Jessica from across the bar. It was time for us to go, so I could put my plan into action. I grabbed her keys, purse, and cell, and started walking to the door. We were waiting for the valet to bring my car, when I looked at her phone, and she had six missed calls from Mike. He probably wanted to know where she was. I threw the cell in her purse with the keys. The guy from inside came outside with three other dudes.

"Yo' my man. I think it's in your best interest to let us take her home. I know her mom, and she is waiting for me to drop her off. I think she is a little too drunk to go home with you. Especially, if she doesn't know your name. I hope this isn't going to be a problem." He said, lifting his shirt to show his piece. I just threw my hand up to say that I surrender.

"Ok Jess. I'll call you tomorrow. I kissed her, slipping my tongue in her mouth. The kiss she gave me was as if I was her man. I can't even lie, my dick was hard as hell. I watched the guys put her in the car and pull off.

Jessica

The baby shower was so much fun until Candace blew my spot up and told everyone I was pregnant. I still couldn't believe that their mom was in jail for murdering their father. Now, I can see why Jas tolerated the abuse Ty was giving her. Domestic Violence is no joke, and men walk around doing that shit to women like it's ok. I was sitting at the front desk of the hospital, when some dude walked in looking for his dad.

He was handsome, tall, brown-skinned, and had a nice build. He slipped me his phone number after I told him I would have a drink, and told me to text me that night, but Mike was home, so I had to wait until the next day. Mike knew something was up, because I shut my phone off and went to bed early. He kept asking if I was mad at him, but I couldn't say anything, because he would know I was hiding something. He rolled me over and tried having sex with me, but I was focused, and I knew that I wouldn't go through with it if he made love to me.

"Jess, what the fuck is up? You never turn me down for sex, and it's not your period, because you're pregnant. I swear to God, it better not be another nigga." He was so mad, but I stuck to my guns and rolled back over. I couldn't sleep, so I went to check on Damien, and he was knocked out. I checked on Mike, and he was knocked out with just his sweats. I had to cover him up and walk away, because that dick print of his had my mouth watering. My thoughts were all over the place, as I saw no sleep last night. I got Damien and myself up the next day, got dressed, and left.

I dropped Damien off at daycare and went about my day without texting Mike. I needed him to think that I was mad at him in order for shit to go down with no interruptions. I didn't hear from Mike all day, and when I got home, he wasn't there, which was good for me. I walked downstairs to my mom's apartment to get her to watch my son.

"Hey, ma? I need you to keep Damien tonight. I'm going out, and Mike will probably be out too." She looked at me and put her hands on her hips.

"Jessy." That's what she calls me. "What is going on with you and Mike? He came down here looking for you. When he didn't see you, he said he was staying at his own house tonight." She said, making my heart stop, because he had been with me every day since that shit with Maria.

"Ma, please. I need you to keep him tonight, and his dad will have him for the rest of the weekend."

"I don't know what's going on with you, but please be safe. You're pregnant, engaged, and have a son. I don't want anything bad to happen to you."

"Thank you." I kissed her on the cheek and left Damien with her. I grabbed his clothes for the night and looked through my closet for an outfit before I text dude.

Him: The guy finally text me the address. I was dressed and on my way.

Me: I'll be there. When I got to the club, I noticed him sitting in the car but kept walking in as if I didn't. I looked around to a few guys and nodded my head. This club was nice and the atmosphere seemed peaceful, but shit could kick off at any time. Dude came behind me saying I looked nice. We danced and had a few drinks that were only water with the olive. I went to the bathroom, when I got a text that something was slipped in my drink, so roll with it.

I came back out, and Marcus fed me some line about drinks are never safe, so he ordered me a new one. I drank the entire thing, and within ten minutes, I pretended to be fucked up. I was falling, slurring my words, and hanging all over him. I had to be extra careful not to piss him off.

Some dude I knew came up to me and asked if I was ok. Marcus told him he had me and that I was ok. It was time to leave when the same guy came out with a few of his friends. They wouldn't let me leave with him, but I let him kiss me.

The guy walked me to the black truck, and we all got in. They watched as Marcus pulled off before turning around to me.

"Girl, that was quite a fucking performance." Jose said, putting the car in drive. I looked over at Joey, hugged him, and told him how much I missed him.

"I'm so glad you didn't tell anyone you were here. I have to do this, and because no one knows who you are, I need you to stay put one more day please." I begged him before sending Mike a text asking where he was.

Me: Hey. Where are you?

"Ok, but I don't want to hear no shit when she finds out I'm home, and you're hogging me to yourself." He said, dropping me back off to my house.

"I love you. Joey, were you able to set everything up for me like I asked?" He just nodded his head.

"Ok, good. I'm going for tomorrow night, but if not, definitely Sunday. I cannot fuck this up." I told him, getting into my new car. Mike text me back as I was putting on my seatbelt.

"I love you too." He said, as they pulled off.

Mike: At the bar playing pool. Why?
Me: I want to see you.
Mike: Oh, now you want to see a nigga. I'm good. I'll talk to you tomorrow.
Me: Word, it's like that? Ok.

I drove my car straight to the bar, got out, and walked in. I sat at the bar next to some older man that started talking my ear off as soon as I sat. Mike was playing pool with Mo and

Darrell and burning a hole in my back. My phone lit up to tell me I had a message.

Mike: Oh, you playing games? Where the fuck is your ring at, and why are you dressed like that?

I looked down at my finger and realized I left it home rushing to get the club. I had to come up with an excuse.

Me: I must've left in on the dresser, after I put my lotion on.

That was the only thing I could think of off the top of my head.

Mike: Come over here.

Me: Ugh no. Remember, you're good. You'll see me tomorrow. I think I'll go home and think about how my fiancé wants to stay in a house where he almost lost me at to his ex. I'm gone. Don't text my ass or look for me. Continue playing your game, I'll see you when I see you.

Just as I was about to leave, Alicia, Candace, Ri Ri, and her husband all walked in looking at me like I was crazy.

"Bitch, what the fuck you doing her dressed like that? I know Mike is pissed." Alicia said, looking at Mike and pointing at my outfit.

"Oh, he didn't tell you. Mike not fucking with me. He told my mom he was staying at his house tonight. I thought that was funny being as though he's been staying with me, so maybe he has plans with someone else." I told her, as she and Candace folded their arms looking at Mike.

See these chics are definitely my sisters, and I wouldn't change that for the world. They turned so quick on Mike, and they knew him longer. Too bad I couldn't tell them what I was up to either. I gave my sisters a hug and sent Ri Ri a text to come outside. I needed to talk to her. I was in the dark ass parking lot so that no one could see us talking if they came out the door.

"Listen. I am going to need you to get everyone together here at the address tomorrow around eight. Do you think you can do that?" I asked her. She nodded her head and stepped out of the car. She and Jas were the only two that knew what I was doing. This was the only way, and Jas had just had a baby, so I couldn't have her put herself out there like that. I sent Jas a text.

Me: It's a go. I love you, sis, and give my niece a kiss for me.

Jas: Be careful. I love you, too, sis. How is Mike handling things?

I went to text her back when Mike knocked on my window. I locked my phone and threw it on the seat. I rolled my window down and kept the door locked. The look in Mike's eye had me nervous as fuck.

"Where the fuck you going?" I just looked at him like he was crazy.

"First of all nigga, don't talk to me like that. You have never spoken to me that way so don't start. Second, I'm grown, and you not feeling me right now, so why does it matter?" He took another pull and passed me the blunt.

"You know what, you're right; I'm sorry, but get this, I'm making you a promise that, if I find out you're cheating on me, I will kill you, him, and me, so before you pull off, I suggest you tell me where you're going." He unlocked the door with his keys, and at that moment, I was mad that I gave him the extra set. He opened the door and turned my body to his so that he was in between my legs. I could tell that he was a little drunk from the liquor on his breath.

"Mike, cut the shit. I'm going to my house, and I need you to listen to me now. If you're not home with me in twenty minutes, I'm coming back out here, find you, and cut this dick right here off." I said, grabbing it through his pants and holding it.

"Oh, yea? You just turning into a gangsta chic now fucking with my sisters." He pulled me closer and unzipped his pants, removed my panties and fucked me right in the parking lot. This was the first time we had sex outside, and the thrill had my adrenaline pumping.

When we were done, I looked at Mike and said, "You got twenty minutes nigga. Don't make me come back out here." When I got to my house, Mike pulled up right behind me. "I looked at him and said, "That's what I thought." And walked upstairs to my apartment.

Tina Jenkins

It was the day to finish what I had started, and I was up and out before Mike again. I packed a bag of clothes, put them in my truck, and went to work. I loved that man so much, but I knew there would be no peace in our world until this was done. I sent a message to Marcus to tell him I would meet him again at the same place and same time. Of course, he started texting me some off the wall shit about coming back to the room with him, so I agreed, knowing that that wasn't happening.

I made sure to exchange messages to Mike all day so he wouldn't become suspicious again and blow my cover. I was now five weeks pregnant, and I knew, damn well, he would've stopped this shit before it got started. I spoke with Jas and Ri Ri all day going over the plan. I got off around one, went to the salon, and told Mike that I was going by Jas' house, and he was ok with that, because they were at Darrell's garage gambling anyway. Jas and Ri Ri helped me get ready, and when I say I was dressed to kill, that was an understatement.

I had my hair washed and curled and my feet and nails done. I put on a small pair of silver hoop earrings, a short black dress, where the cleavage was opened in the front with some six-inch black stiletto Louboutin heels that Mike bought me for Christmas. Ri Ri did my makeup. Shit, I would say I looked like J-Lo with a short haircut. I told Jas to snap some pictures, because I didn't usually dress like that, and it was nice to see. Jas had only been out the hospital for a week, but she refused to miss this, and I didn't blame her.

She and Ri Ri dressed in all black and sent the text message out for everyone to meet at a certain address. I told her to put 911 at the end of the group message so everyone knew it was serious. Ms. D came upstairs to get the baby, and we left. It was about 8:15 when we got to the address. Joey, Jose, and the rest of the guys got out the truck. I introduced them to Jas, and Ri Ri, took a deep breath and opened the door to see everyone sitting at the table. Mike was talking to Darrell, but when he saw me holding hands with Joey, he pointed his gun right at his head. Shit got out of hand so fast.

Mike

Ever since I proposed to Jess, she had been acting funny like she fucking with somebody else. I already told her that, if she ever cheated on me, I was snapping her fucking neck, and I wasn't playing. I didn't give this girl my heart, my seeds, my ring, and about to give her my last name, for her to fuck around.

"Jess, what's up? You mad at me for something?" I asked her, but she rolled over, not talking to me. I don't know what the hell going on, but I sure as hell ain't sleeping in here with her acting like that. I took my ass in the living room and copped a squat on the couch. I laid back, looking up at the ceiling, when I decided to scroll through my photos and videos. I came across the video of me proposing to Jess and seeing how happy she was, I doubt if she was cheating, but I was going to give her a taste of her medicine tomorrow.

I woke up, and they were gone already, so I made me a bowl of cereal, got dressed, and went downstairs. I loved talking to her mom, because she was down to earth and always told me how she felt without cursing. We ended up talking for two hours about her son, who was in jail, and her other daughter, who was killed by a hit and run driver ten years ago. I mean, damn, Jess never told me all this stuff. I guess she was embarrassed.

"Why didn't Jess tell me this?" I asked her, and she looked at me and said,

"Jessy was driving the car when her sister was killed, but the other driver was the one drunk. Jessy had just turned seventeen and had gotten her license, but Linda was teaching her how to drive. They were only two years apart, and she idolized Linda. It was one in the afternoon, when a drunk driver ran the red light and t-boned the car, killing Linda on impact. Jess was in the hospital for weeks, because the car was pushed into a tree on her side. Jessy missed Linda's funeral and blamed herself.

She said that she should've been the one dead, because Linda was the one who usually drove. She couldn't forgive herself and never spoke of it again. I had to take all Linda's pictures down, because Jess would have a break down each time she looked at one. I wear this locket with Linda's picture on it, so I will have her with me wherever I go. I know I shouldn't have gave in and kept the pictures, but I hated to see her crying. She will tell you when she's ready, but don't force it out of her.

"Wow, that's crazy. What happened to your son? Why is he in jail?" I asked, waiting to hear what happened, but she said that Jess wasn't afraid to talk about that and that I needed to ask her. We talked a little while longer, and I told her that I would see her tomorrow, because I was staying at home. I knew it would piss Jess off, but she deserved it after the way she was acting.

She text me around 11:30, asking me where I was. I told her at the bar and that I would see her tomorrow, but her ass showed up in a skintight mini dress. She was looking good as hell, but where the fuck was she coming from dressed like that? I know dam well she didn't go out with Candace and Alicia, because they all were on their way here. I sent her a few messages while she sat in the bar. She was sending me messages talking shit. I saw her get up to leave, when my sisters walked in, and she turned them against me just that quick. I watched her leave, and I went to take a piss before going out there to make sure she left.

She had the door locked, when I knocked on the window. She thought that I didn't know she was texting someone, but that was ok, because all would reveal itself. I unlocked the door, pulled her close, and fucked her right in the parking lot. I didn't care who saw us; she was about to be my wife. She threatened my ass, too, telling me to be home in twenty minutes, and I knew she was serious. She had been hanging around my sisters too long, and they turned her into a gangsta bitch.

I woke up the next day, and she was already gone again, but she text me all day telling me how much she loved and missed me. I'm no fool; something wasn't right, but that was ok. I was going to find out soon enough. The last text I got from her was that she would be at my brother's house, and to pick her up on my way home from the shop. While we were all in the shop, we got this message from Ri Ri saying we needed to have an emergency meeting around eight at the address she sent.

When we got there, it looked like it was an old abandoned house on the outside, but when you walked in, it was fully furnished. There was a huge dining room table with twelve seats, and that's where we all sat. It was 8:15 when the door opened, and we heard some clicking of heels walking down the hall. I looked at Jas and Ri Ri walk in wearing all black, but when I saw Jess walk in looking like a fucking model, holding some nigga's hand, I lost it. I pulled my 9mm out and aimed it right at his head. Everybody jumped up pulling out their shit, when the other dudes she walked in with pulled out their guns.

"Jess, you got fucking five seconds to tell me why you dressed like that and walking in here holding this nigga's hand. She looked at me, rolled her eyes, and moved my arm down, so that the gun was pointing at her. I could hear Jas and Ri Ri screaming for me to calm down.

"Baby, if you're going to kill me, then go ahead, but I won't allow you to kill my brother. He just came home, and I don't think my mom will be happy that she didn't get to see him first. I told you, I would never cheat on you, and you doubted my trust, and because of that, I don't want you coming to my house tonight. Everything that I'm doing is for us to have peace, and the first thing you thought I was doing was dipping out." After she said that shit, I was pissed.

"Shit, you didn't even tell me you had a fucking brother. I found that shit out today from your mom. Maybe, if you didn't shut me out, I wouldn't feel like this." I told her, now getting mad that everybody could hear us arguing. No one said a word, as they pretended to be looking down at their phones or talking about other shit.

"Nigga, that's strike two. I told your ass don't ever speak to me like that again. I have never disrespected you since we been together, and I expect the same from you. There's a lot of shit you don't know about me. If you keep going, I swear to God I won't marry you. Now, test me if you fucking want to. You can sit there and be mad all damn night or listen to what I have to say. I called everyone here, because I need all of your help." I couldn't do shit but walk out.

I stood outside smoking when her brother came out to introduce himself. He told me that I needed to come inside to hear what she had to say, because she was going to need me tonight. I apologized to him about pulling a gun out on him.

"Shit, if my girl walked in looking like that with a dude, holding his hand, I would've done the same fucking thing. I thought you were going to really shoot me until she walked up to you. I don't know what my sister did to you, but at least, I know you would kill or die for her. And that's the kind of guy she needs in her corner, so let's go in here so you can hear what she has to say."

I walked back in as Jess gave a brief description of what happened to her sister, but what she said next had me shocked as hell. She described how her and her brother found the woman that killed her sister. They killed her, the husband, the daughter, the son, and the dog. They set the house on fire and watched it burn. The neighbors said they saw two kids running from the house. They found Joey and not me, because his ass wanted to go to the store, and I went home. They knew that it was two of us, but Joey took the weight. They gave him ten years for Arson but couldn't charge him with the murders, because they couldn't find the gun.

We were all looking at each other like, not Jess, she was too scary for all that. I guess, when it comes to family, you toughen up and do what you had to do. She said she would explain the rest later, because the time was ticking, and she had to get on the road.

Once she told us the plan, I yelled out, "Hell no, Jess. You are pregnant, and I am not having you lose the babies again." She walked from around the table over to me with that look that makes my dick hard. I could see everybody watching us.

"Baby, I'm glad you got out of your feelings, but Jas can't do it. She's only been out the hospital for a week. You can ride with my brothers to keep me safe, but you have to stay out of sight. I promise, I won't let him hurt us." She said, putting her arms around my neck and throwing her tongue down my throat.

"Jess, I'm not comfortable with this for real, and that kiss is not making me change my mind." She pulled me closer and whispered in my ear that she promised to do certain things with her mouth she knew I loved. I asked Joey what truck they were taking after she said that, making everybody laugh.

"That is my bitch right there." Alicia said, slapping hands with all the girls. I watched her walk back around the table and tell everybody what they needed to do. She sent a message to the guy, Marcus, to tell him she was on her way. She came back by me and pulled me outside.

"I love you with all my heart, and I trust you to keep me safe, but I need for you to stay calm at all times. If you see something,you don't like, look down at the video of you proposing to me, and remember that I'm doing this for Jas, Ri Ri, Alicia, our babies, and us. I love you, Mike, and please don't let anything happen to me." She said, giving me a kiss and walking to her truck.

"Jess, I love you too. I swear, if I think for one minute you're not safe, I'm stepping in right away." I told her, closing the door.

"I wouldn't have it any other way."

We hopped in her brother's truck and followed behind her to the club but kept a safe distance. I was dying when she stepped out to walk in that club without me looking like that. Her brother had some other people inside watching, and since the bartender was their cousin, he let them put a camera in the club earlier. The music was so loud that I couldn't hear what she was saying to him, but he was feeling all over her body. He started kissing her neck and then her lips. She walked to the bathroom, and this nigga stuck something in her drink, and I had had enough. I tried to get out, but Mo and Joey kept me in the truck.

She sent me a text from the bathroom telling me she loved me and to keep her safe. I told her that he put something in her drink, but she knew already. Their cousin already switched the drinks before he turned back around. I watched her walk out the bathroom, kiss him, and pass the pill to her cousin. He stuck it in his drink and stirred it, tapping Jess that he was finished. She stopped kissing him and started sipping on her drink and watching him drink his. He drank all that shit, and I hoped he felt the effects soon, because I was getting tired of watching my fiancé with another man.

They started dancing, when we noticed him wobbling and barely able to stand. It was Jose and his friend's turn to play their part. They walked in, as if they were bouncers, asking him if he was ok. They walked him out to the truck, looked around, and put him into the trunk.

Jess walked out the club, hugging me tightly, and not letting go. She laid her head on my shoulder and squeezed my hand, as we headed back to the house we were at earlier. "Baby, text Jas and tell them we are on the way." She picked her phone up and sent the message out so everyone would be ready when we got there.

Jasmine

The day after I gave birth to Harmony, Jess came up to my room when she got off work to tell me she saw Ty's ass. He came in asking for the room that his dad was in and ended up asking for her number. She told Ty some bullshit ass story about catching Mike out there, cheating so it was ok for her to do the same. Jess told me that she knew who he was from the last time he beat on me, and it was now payback time. She and I both thought it was taking the guys too long, and it was time to act. I called up Ri Ri, who was staying at the Hilton with her husband for the next two weeks. She came over, and within twenty minutes, came up with the best plan ever. We knew to keep this to ourselves, because Candace and Alicia would slip up or the guys would say no.

The first night Jess went out with him, I was so nervous, because I knew she could get hurt, and Mike would kill me. I was going to send Ri Ri over there with her, but I was afraid that she would blow her cover. Jess assured me that she picked her brother up from jail the day before and were planning to surprise her mom. Once she told him what happened with the babies and everything else, he was all for it. They had a cousin that worked as a bartender and would be feeding her water drinks that looked like Martini's. Jess told me everything she was going to do, and it was a great plan.

She text me that night and told me all was good but filled me and Ri Ri in on play for play the next day.

Tonight was the night to finally get this nigga, but we had to be extra careful and couldn't make any mistakes. She came to my house to get dressed, and Ri Ri and I basically had her looking like J-Lo when it was time to go. Mike was going to be pissed, because he hated to see her going out showing so much skin. He felt like no one should see what he was getting and some things should be left for imagination. Ms. D came and got the baby from me, giving all of us a kiss and said be safe, but get that nigga. She was so gangsta for an old woman.

Joey and his cousins were parked outside the address we were going to when she introduced us, and come to find out, he was her brother. We really didn't know a lot about Jess, but when this shit was over, we were making her tell us her life story. Jess walked in nervous, so Joey took her hand to try and calm her nerves. We walked in the house straight to the dining room where everyone was. I saw Mike look at Jess, then at Joey and their hands, at that was it. Mike went ballistic pulling his gun out and shit. Jess didn't even flinch; she just lowered his arm with the gun in it and pointed at herself.

I have to admit, though, she snapped on Mike twice putting him in his place, and I had nothing but respect for her after that. She wasn't playing any games with allowing a man to disrespect her, and if Mike didn't know before, he knew now. He got so mad that he just left until Jess looked at her brother for him to go get him.

"Since my fiancé is in his feelings, I am going to tell you why I brought you guys here." She said, starting to talk, when Mike walked back in, becoming mad all over again, after she explained what was going to happen. We all thought they were going to have another argument. Instead, she walked up to him, kissing him and whispering something probably nasty in his ear calming him the fuck down. She had definitely made him a better man, and she had his ass sprung.

We watched Jess leave the house and finished setting up the house for them to show up. Jess didn't go out with Ty the first day, because her brother Joey had to help get everything the way we needed to pull this off. Joey's girlfriend allowed them to use her house for the next few days. Her brother had cameras put up all over the house; he left guns in each closet of the house, and set the basement up for the best part. We checked to make sure the sound worked on the cameras and got in position when she called to tell me that they were on their way.

"Ok, everybody, they should be here in twenty minutes, so get in your positions." I told them, looking at Alicia, who was not moving.

"Alicia, what's wrong? Why aren't you in the shed to watch the video?"

"I want to see this nigga up close and personal and fuck him up for all the shit he put us through."

I took the blunt, took a pull, and blew the smoke in the air. I knew the feeling that she was having, because I couldn't wait myself for them to get there. This was all of our chance to get his ass back for what he did to all of us.

"Alicia, you will have your turn to do that, but if he walks in and sees you, he will know it's a set up. We have to stick to the plan, or Jess will have put herself out there for nothing." I told her, pulling her off the couch and taking her to the basement. Cordell walked in, and Alicia ran to him crying, because she couldn't believe this was about to be over. We heard the cars pull up, turned all the lights off, and took our positions.

The guys took him out the car, brought him up the stairs and into the house. They sat him on the couch, as he laid there hunched over. It was only 1:15 when they got back, and no one knew how long that drug was going to have his ass sleep.

"Yo', I have one of those Narcan shot things that wake people up from overdoses. We can try that to get him up." Jose said, looking around. We all shrugged our shoulders like ok and waited for him to come back with it. When he came back in, Jess looked at Mike, blew her breath, and got ready to put on a show.

Jess shot the Narcan needle thing in his arm when he slowly woke up. I watched Jess walk from the kitchen bringing him some water like a good housewife. She told him he passed out at the bar, and when he asked where they were, she said her brother's girlfriend's house. He needed the bathroom, so Jess walked him to the back and pointed to it. I could see fire coming from Mike's ears, and she hadn't even done the hardest part yet.

"Hey. How are you holding up?" I asked him not expecting the answer.

"I can't believe you knew about this shit and agreed with her to do it. Jas, I would never let Mo put you in harm's way." I couldn't do anything but sit there with my mouth open when Mo stepped in.

"Look, bro, I know this is hard to watch, but don't take it out on Jasmine. She told me she offered to do it, but Jess wanted to hurry up and be rid of this nigga. Jas just had the baby, and she knew that it would just take longer, and who knew when he would come back."

"I know Jas, and I'm sorry. I just can't stand to watch her put herself in harm's way. I know y'all think we were taking our time, but the shit kept being put off for the accident, you having the baby, and so forth. Yea, I could've sent someone to get him, but it's not the same as doing it yourself. People make mistakes, and I couldn't take the chance of that happening." He said, not taking his eyes off the screen.

"Mike, you don't have to watch this. You know it's too many of us here that won't allow anything happen. She trusts you the most, and that's why she went in there with so much confidence. We all know as well as her that you won't let him do any more damage to her. You have to trust that she knows what she's doing and have faith. I don't know how many times we have to say that." I told him, as he put his finger up telling me to wait. When I looked at the screen, he pulled her down on the couch with him. Shit hit the fan after that.

Jessica

After we got back from the club and dropped him on the couch, I couldn't stay away from Mike. I was scared I wouldn't be able to fight him off if he did something before they could get to me. He kept whispering in my ear trying to calm me down, but it wasn't working.

"The only thing that could keep me calm right now, baby, is putting a bullet through his head and go home. I don't understand why you're doing all this extra shit." I ignored him putting my game face on.

"Ok, it's time, baby. Watch me, and don't come unless I call you ok." It took him a few minutes to wake up and realize that we weren't at the club anymore. He started asking questions like where was he, and how did he get there? I told him that he passed out from all the shots he took and security walked him to my car. He seemed to be ok with the answer when he excused himself to the bathroom. I knew that he was checking his surroundings, so I waited on the couch for him to come back.

"Hey, so we're here now. What's up?" I asked him, as he was looking on his phone.

"You tell me. This isn't your house you said, so I mean how much can we really do here?" He asked me, letting me know he wanted to fuck.

"Oh, don't worry about my brother's girlfriend. She doesn't care as long as I clean up whatever mess I make. I hope you would help me make a mess." I said, smiling at him. He pulled me closer by the neck kissing me hungrily like he was in a rush. I pulled away for a second to ask,

"Do you have any condoms?" He reached inside his wallet and pulled out a magnum one. I knew he didn't need that shit from what Jas told me. He took his shirt off and laid me down on the couch, rubbing on my legs and grinding on my body. He opened my dress and tried to slide my panties down.

"Yo', what's up with that?" He asked, sliding his hand down my leg trying to pull them down again.

"You know what? I thought I could do this, but I can't." I told him, when he grabbed my arms and put them above my head. I tried to wiggle out of his embrace, but he was too strong. I knew that everyone was about to bust through the doors, so I had to calm him down before they blew the whole shit.

"Ok, Ok." I said, kissing him and making him release my arms. I was able to push him up a little, giving myself more room to scoot up. I was able to sit all the way up when he flipped.

"Yo', what the fuck you doing? Stop playing games." I put my hand up to the camera signaling for them not to come in yet.

"I don't think I'm ready to go that far with you yet. I mean, we just met." I told him. He started getting mad and yelling about me playing games. Talking about I shouldn't have brought him home if I wasn't going to give it to him. I stood up fixing my clothes, when he grabbed my arm throwing me on the couch.

"I'm done playing these games with you." He said, as we were tussling. I was able to get on my feet, when he got up behind me turning me around to face him.

"I want you to take all your clothes off." He said, and what happened to Jas, immediately popped in my mind.

"Hell no, nigga. I said I wasn't ready, and I'm not fucking you. I'll call you a cab, and you can wait outside for it. I walked to the bookshelf, grabbed the phone to call a cab, when he put his hand up to hit me. I pulled the 9mm off the shelf and pointed it straight at him. He was so busy trying to fuck that he didn't even notice that it was left out in plain sight. Mike showed me where it was before he left just in case shit got out of hand before he could save me.

"What the fuck you going to do with that?" He was shaking his head laughing. I didn't find shit funny.

"I want to do to you what you did to my babies and family, but I have something for that ass." He looked scared that I knew who he really was. I kept the gun pointed at him, as I told him to go down in the basement. When he got down there, he looked amazed, because it was set up like a bedroom. There was a full sized bed, a video camera set up, some candles lit, some handcuffs, duct tape, rope, a shovel, a chainsaw, and other tools we planned on using.

Just as he turned around to say something, Jasmine walked out of the shadows with Ri Ri. His eyes got big as saucers.

"Marissa, is that you?" Looking at her, then at Jas, probably not realizing how much they resembled one another.

"Yes, it's me motherfucker, and it took me a while to get to you, but I'm here." She pushed him down on the bed and started kissing him, when she bit down on his tongue, causing blood to escape his mouth instantly.

"What the fuck you do that for?" She just got up, held her hand out for the gun that I was holding and pistol whipped him knocking him back on the bed. We started undressing him, placing the handcuffs around his hands, put duck tape on his mouth, laid him on his stomach. Then, we turned on the video camera and watched Rodney take his ass. Now, Rodney was gay, and he had full-blown aids and was horny as hell. He was our childhood friend, and when I told him what he did to Jas and Ri Ri, he wanted to help.

Alicia and Candace walked in the room smoking a blunt watching Rodney rape Ty. They all sat there smoking and watching, while I just inhaled the smoke, because I knew that Mike would kick my ass if I touched it. Rodney raped Ty for almost an hour in every position possible and no one said a word. It was like Jas and Marissa needed to see this happen to him. Ty woke up in between some of it screaming and squirming, and Rodney got aggravated, so he was pistol whipped again. After Rodney told us he had no more use for him, he helped us sit him in the chair. Alicia took some water and threw it in his face waking him up.

Marissa walked over with a machete, pulled his dick from in between his legs, and cut that shit right off. We wanted him to die a slow death, so I made sure to do research which is why we stuck a balled up towel over it and had him sit on a bag of ice. Jas took the machete from Marissa, walked over to him, and cut off both of his hands. I tied tourniquets around the wrist area to try and keep him from dying. We could tell that he was slowly fading, but Alicia hadn't gotten her revenge yet. She took the gun and shot him in both kneecaps.

"I want to make sure you can't even walk in hell motherfucker." Marissa and Jas both walked up to him to ask the same question.

I held his head up for them and Marissa asked first, "Why?" He just started laughing and spitting out blood. Jas stood next to him and asked him next, and he shocked us with the answer.

"I hated you Jasmine for fucking that nigga and you were supposed to be mines. I felt bad so I came back for you. You are my soul mate."

"Are you fucking kidding me? Do you know what you did to us? Do you even care? Jas started punching on him, and he just kept laughing. Marissa took the gasoline that she found in the basement and sprayed it on his feet and lit a match. He started screaming, but it didn't matter, because I picked up the machete, lifted his neck, and cut his head off.

Tina Jenkins

Mike

When Jess blew her breath before they woke that nigga up, I knew she was scared. I led her to the bookshelf and told her I was leaving my gun just in case something happened, and we couldn't get to her in time. She put her arms around my neck, kissed me, and said, "Baby, it's just about over."

I hated looking at the shit taking place, but she was right; this shit needed to be over. I was so proud of her when she grabbed that gun and let him know who she was. The fear in his face was priceless. Everything that happened to him after that was what he deserved. From the rape, to getting his dick cut off and set on fire. But the best part was when my girl showed me how gangsta she was when she decapitated his ass. I guess, when he made her lose our babies that shit did something to her, but then again, she'd been gangsta. She hid that shit well from all of us, but that was ok, because I refused to ever let her do anything like that again.

Here we are now, and a year went by since that shit happened with Ty and the girls. I still couldn't believe that I watched my soon to be wife cut a man's head off in front of me. That was some shit straight out of the movies, but to this day, ain't nobody fucking with our clique. Marissa and her husband moved to Jersey to start a new life. Of course, he transferred here, and they became the Godparents of our twins, Mike Junior (MJ) and Aria. Yes, Jess ended up pregnant with twins the second time around. Even though He had our first two angels, he blessed us with two more.

I watched Candace, Alicia, Marissa, Malika, and Jas walked down the aisle before Jess stepped out. She walked out wearing a champagne wedding dress with a six-foot train. She looked so beautiful; when she got to the altar, she wiped my eyes, as I did the same to her. I lifted the veil up, kissing her before the pastor could say we are gathered here today. Mo and Jas pulled us back so the pastor could start. She reached over and wiped the lipstick off my mouth. Before we did our first dance, I wanted to get the toast me and my wife made for each other out of the way.

"A year-and-a-half ago, my wife changed my life when she said yes to marry me. I didn't think I deserved someone as perfect as she was. She made me a better man, a better father because I had no idea to do with newborns, let alone, two at a time. We saw each other through the roughest times and the best of times. There's no woman out here that I want in my life more than you; unless it's my daughter, then you have competition." I toasted making everyone laugh.

"I was hurt so bad in the past, and I never thought I would find someone to love me as much as you did. I wake up every day thanking God that he placed you in my life. I knew that you were made for me when you took my son as your own and didn't push him to the side if we had a disagreement. I will always love you and Devon for bringing so much joy to our lives. Baby, thank you for choosing me to hold you down and spend the rest of your life with." She said, letting a teardrop before the DJ called us out for the first dance.

Boy, I never knew a love like you before,
You came into my life and gave me more,
You are my friend, also my man,
And I'll love you always,

"Always" by Pebbles blasted through the speakers as we danced and kissed. She would sing the words to me. I saw Jas, Mo, Candace, Darrell, Alicia, Cornell, Marissa, and Mario all come out to the dance floor halfway through the song. I didn't mind, because they were all my family now in one way or another.

Text Shan to 22828 to stay up to date with new releases, sneak peeks, contest, and more...
Or sign up Here
Check your spam if you don't receive an email thanking you for signing up.

CPSIA information can be obtained at www.ICGtesting.com
Printed in the USA
LVOW10s1315270716

497997LV00028B/658/P